FOR MIMI & CJ
- ROBIN

FOR EMELIE & NATALIE
- JAN

FREAKY & FEARLESS

How to Tell a Tall Tale

ROBIN ETHERINGTON

ILLUSTRATED BY JAN BIELECKI

Piccadilly
PRESS

First published in Great Britain in 2016 by
PICCADILLY PRESS
80–81 Wimpole St, London W1G 9RE
www.piccadillypress.co.uk

A CIP catalogue record for this book is available from the British
Library.

ISBN: 978-1-8481-2510-0
also available as an ebook

1

Printed and bound by Clays Ltd, St Ives Plc

MIX
Paper from
responsible sources
FSC
www.fsc.org
FSC® C018072

Piccadilly Press is an imprint of Bonnier Publishing Fiction,
a Bonnier Publishing company
www.bonnierpublishingfiction.co.uk
www.bonnierpublishing.co.uk

ISSUE #2286

ACTION!
DANGER!
LAUGHS!

DINNER IS
SERVED! NEW
BATTY BEASTS
ADVENTURE
INSIDE

BATTY BEASTS

ONCE THERE LIVED A CHEF WHO DREAMED OF MAKING THE BEST-SMELLING, BEST-TASTING SOUP EVER.

IN HIS DESIRE FOR FAME, HE IGNORED THE WARNINGS OF OTHER CHEFS.

GAH! TOO SMELLY!

MY NOSE IS CRYING!

HIS SOUP WAS SO PUNGENT IT COULD BE DETECTED IN SPACE!

POOEY!

BRAVE DINERS CAME FROM ALL OVER, JUST FOR A SNUFFLE.

I'M GOING IN!

BUT THE GREAT PONG ATTRACTED A FIEND WITH A NOSE FOR TROUBLE.

THE BEAST ATTACKED, SEARCHING FOR THE SOURCE OF THE SCANDALOUS STINK.

FEARING FOR HIS LIFE, THE CHEF FLED THE COUNTRY.

UNDERWEAR, SOCKS, WORLD'S MOULDIEST CHEESE...

BUT TO HIS HORROR, THE BEAST GAVE CHASE!

CHAPTER 1

A FREAKY FAREWELL

Soup so stinky you could smell it in space, an unstoppable shadowy beast and a showdown on a waterfall . . .

Simon Moss placed last week's comic on his knees and let out a long sigh.

Wow. That's how you start a story, he thought.

Simon leaned back against his pillow

and stared up at the ceiling of his bedroom. Last year he'd saved up three months' worth of pocket money in order to buy enough glow-in-the-dark stars to cover his entire ceiling with all the constellations of the northern sky. Well, his dad had done most of the actual sticking. Simon's eleven-year-old arms couldn't quite reach that far, and he'd been banned from balancing on the back of chairs after one tiny chair-breaking accident that could have happened to pretty much anyone.

Outside, the summer sun was beating down, but all morning Simon had kept his curtains closed and the light on in order to charge the phosphorescence that made the stars glow. Feeling to his left, he flicked off the light switch. The starry ceiling seemed to shine brighter than ever.

Simon had always loved space. It was one great big, endless mystery. Anything could be happening out there. If there was a chance there might actually be alien life on other planets then it also seemed entirely possible that astronauts might be able to smell soup among the stars.

Simon frowned. The **FEARLESS** adventures were certainly more likely to take place in space than in the town of Lake Shore. The only event in Simon's world today was a pretty gloomy one. He'd known it was coming for weeks but finally the day had arrived. His dad was leaving to go away on business for the first time ever, and Simon didn't even know where he was headed. 'Oh, nowhere important' had been his dad's reply, which wasn't very helpful.

There was a knock at his bedroom door, which opened before Simon could say anything. Parents had a strange habit of doing that, he thought. Why knock if you're just going to come in anyway?

His dad entered the room, then stopped and blinked rapidly in the half light.

'Midday outside, and midnight indoors. Interesting. Inspiration for another of your tall tales?'

Simon loved making up stories. He loved writing them, loved reading them, and he loved sharing them. The more exciting and original, the better. He wasn't sure where the ideas came from but he'd never been short of a good story, or 'tall tale', as his dad liked to call them.

His dad smiled and sat down on the edge of the bed next to Simon.

'Ah, is that last week's issue? You know,

I haven't read it yet.'

He took **FEARLESS** from Simon's knee and began to read. It still amazed Simon that his dad enjoyed comics. He'd bought Simon his very first issues, and always made the time to read them, before asking Simon lots of questions about the heroes and villains that filled the pages. Lately he had been particularly interested in the *Batty Beasts* stories, and pretty much anything featuring monsters.

'Beast attacks,' said his dad, as he passed the comic back. 'Hard to predict when or where they'll happen. Tricky for an adult . . . impossible for a young boy!'

And with that, he pounced and began tickling his son in the ribs until tears of laughter rolled down Simon's cheeks.

'I surrender,' said Simon, gasping for breath. 'I surrender!'

His dad nodded and let him go.

'Good choice. The smart adventurer knows when to fight, when to run and when to call it a day.'

Simon looked at his dad again. His usual cheerful mood had been replaced with a thoughtful expression. The stars above them seemed to dim a little as he spoke.

'Listen, Simon. I have a request for you

before I leave. I need your help with something serious.'

Serious. Ah. Whenever his parents used the word 'serious' (a word that no eleven year old finds exciting at the best of times) Simon's overactive imagination would come to his rescue. If his mum said he needed to take his homework seriously, Simon would conjure a mighty castle in his mind, then raise the drawbridge so the dreaded army of Homework could not defeat him. If his dad put him in charge of the lawnmower and said the back garden seriously needed cutting, Simon would imagine himself on a hovercraft skimming over a wild green sea, chopping the tops off the waves with his magnificent machine. His imagination helped make the ordinary extraordinary.

'If you see anything weird,' his dad continued, 'and I mean really weird, let me

know. Anything out of the ordinary.'

'By weird do you mean "Lake Shore FC winning a match" weird, or "dead rising from the grave" weird?' asked Simon.

'Either! That mind of yours is precisely what I'm looking for. When seen through the eyes of a child, the world seems pretty odd, and that's because it *is* odd. And you're special, Simon. You've got the gift of storytelling.'

His dad walked over to Simon's desk and picked up a bright red notebook from the top of the biggest stack. It contained a cowboy/sci-fi story Simon had written called 'Black Day in Death Laser Canyon'. There were lots of cowboys and lots of lasers and a big battle. The lasers won.

His dad turned to him and waggled the notebook.

'All these stories you've written.

Hundreds of them. They're great, Simon, and getting better all the time. I bet you could conjure an adventure from something as dull as a garden gnome, or a wellington boot.'

His dad walked back to the bed and pressed a small piece of paper into Simon's hand. On it was an email address – fearlessfather@farfaraway.world.com.

'You can reach me here while I'm gone. This way we'll be able to chat in secret. Keep your eyes peeled, Simon. Remember, anything peculiar, no matter how silly, write to me. I've a funny feeling we're going to

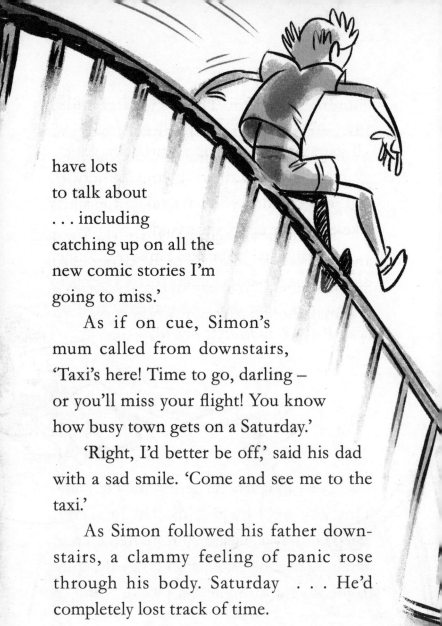

have lots
to talk about
. . . including
catching up on all the
new comic stories I'm
going to miss.'

As if on cue, Simon's
mum called from downstairs,
'Taxi's here! Time to go, darling –
or you'll miss your flight! You know
how busy town gets on a Saturday.'

'Right, I'd better be off,' said his dad
with a sad smile. 'Come and see me to the
taxi.'

As Simon followed his father downstairs, a clammy feeling of panic rose
through his body. Saturday . . . He'd
completely lost track of time.

Simon dodged round his dad, jumped onto the banister, slid down it, and landed on all fours at the feet of his surprised mother.

'Nice of you to wave your father off, but why couldn't you have taken the stairs like everyone else?' she asked.

'Yeah, why?' repeated Simon's younger sister, Ruby, who seemed to be trying to climb into their dad's suitcase. 'Why' was Ruby's favourite word, as in

'Why can't humans fly?', 'Why can't I stick my finger in the plug socket?' and 'Why is it wrong to poo in public?'

Simon actually thought his little sister was cool. Ruby was funny, she liked joining in with Simon's games and she was pretty brave, especially for a four year old. Okay, so her bedroom looked like a bomb had exploded in a paint factory, she

borrowed his action figures without asking, and she had a nasty habit of covering his comics with jam . . . but none of that stuff was important.

Simon didn't answer Ruby. His mind was somewhere else entirely.

He waved as his dad picked up his suitcase, dropped a kiss on his wife's cheek, saluted the children, and got into the taxi. But Simon was on autopilot. He was waving goodbye but he had barely noticed his father waving back.

What if it's REALLY busy in town, he thought. *Or aliens choose this precise moment to invade?*

'Mum, I've got to run to the shops!'

'Simon, your father is leaving.'

Some strange kid might get the last one!

Simon tugged at his mother's arm in desperation.

'But Muuuuum – I've got to go . . .'

He had to go and he had to go now, or they might be sold out and for the first time in his life he would be too late to get his hands on a copy of **FEARLESS** and the world as he knew it would come to an end and . . .

Oh.

24

Simon stood and stared at the empty driveway for what seemed like a lifetime but was only actually about five minutes. His mother and Ruby were still with him, although Ruby was busying herself by burying some of their dad's precious golf balls beneath the front lawn, then rubbing the dirt on her face like some sort of camouflage.

Simon decided to break the silence.

'So, er, when's Dad coming back?'

His mother gave him a look.

'Simon, we talked about this. Your father's going to be away for three months. I'm afraid it's just you, me and Ruby for the summer.'

Oh, thought Simon again. Three months. The entire summer holiday, which was pretty much for ever in Simon's mind. What could possibly take three months? It occurred to Simon again that not only did he not know where his dad was going, but he really didn't have a clue what his dad actually did for a job. It was something to do with the government and science or something, and although Simon loved space, science had never been one of his strong subjects. But standing in the empty drive he found himself regretting not asking his dad more questions, even if he couldn't understand the answers. And he really regretted that when his dad had said he'd miss his comics, Simon hadn't said, 'I'll miss you too'.

He looked at the crumpled email address he still held in his hand. What was it his dad had asked Simon to do? Keep an eye out for anything weird? Well, there was absolutely nothing weird about the town of Lake Shore, pondered Simon. Lake Bore, more like. He'd lived there his whole life and nothing even remotely interesting had ever happened.

But there was one thing he could do for his dad. Simon's dad had asked him to share all the latest comic stories, and to do that Simon would have to get his hands on the brand new copy of **FEARLESS**.

CHAPTER 2

CASTLE FEARLESS

Simon shouted a quick 'BYE!' to his mum and sprinted away, down the pathway of number 40, Stapleton Drive and out onto the pavement.

'Just make sure you're back by lunchtime, Simon,' she shouted from the doorstep. 'You're babysitting Ruby this afternoon, remember?'

Simon added this fact to a growing list

of important things he'd completely forgotten about, but he wasn't going to let it stop him now.

'Yep, sure! How could I forget? See you later!'

And Simon ran. He ran like his life depended on it, his legs pumping faster than ever before. The other houses on his street whistled past as Simon hurtled onwards, the scenery blurring in his mind as he pictured himself reaching a super-sonic sprinting speed.

Simon lived out on the very edge of town, which meant he had a long way to travel for his weekly comic. Normally this wouldn't bother him. In fact, this weekly journey was usually a pleasure because his route took him right past the entrance to the castle, and if Simon's generally dull town had one remarkable feature, it was Castle Fearless.

Hidden behind tall wrought-iron gates, protected by a dozen security cameras, and tucked away at the end of a ridiculously long drive, Castle Fearless was a marvel. It was also, most importantly, the headquarters of the **FEARLESS** comic empire.

As Simon passed the entrance he couldn't help but slow down, until he was jogging on the spot. He stared through the bars of the great gates that stretched up to the sky like metal stalagmites. Even at this

distance, the main building gave new meaning to the word 'huge'. It had been rebuilt years ago, stone by stone, from a pile of crumbling ruins. Parapets now lined every wall and numerous towers crowded against each other, as if struggling and squabbling over which was tallest.

Storming Castle Fearless would take an army, thought Simon. A big one too. You'd probably need ogres. And siege cannon. It was pretty much the perfect place in which to create the greatest comic in the world.

Gazing up at the building he noticed a curtain twitch in a window on the fourth floor.

Simon was stunned. He'd never actually seen anyone enter or leave the building. Nor

had any of his friends, for that matter. Not even the tiniest glimpse, and they'd all spent a long time looking. The two most popular rumours at Simon's school were that there was either a secret entrance to the castle hidden somewhere in town, or – Simon's personal favourite – that the comic artists were all chained up in the dungeon so they could never leave their drawing boards.

As Simon stared, the curtain twitched again. Well, that couldn't be an artist, thought Simon. Not on the fourth floor. No one kept a dungeon on the fourth floor. That would just be silly.

Grabbing the bars of the gate, Simon leaned forward and strained to get a better look. The building was, after all, a very long way away. He couldn't make out any details,

someone watching him?

omething pulled at his shoelaces.
 pping back from the bars he looked
down and came face to button nose with a
very strange animal cowering on the other
side of the gates. It looked a little bit like a
monkey. Well, it had a tail and was furry,
but that was where the similarity stopped.

Simon had never seen anything like it
before, but guessed that if you could afford
to live in a castle, well, you could probably
afford to keep exotic creatures as pets.

The creature made a sort of mewing
noise. It must have reached through the bars
to grab him. Simon knelt down to look at it
more closely. The little thing seemed scared,
which wasn't surprising, as Simon was about
four times its size. He tried to make himself
appear smaller and less threatening.

'Hey, little Gubbin, you don't need to

be scared,' said Simon, stretching out to give the animal a stroke. He ruffled the fur between two bat-like ears. It felt like running his hand across the edge of a book, like paper flicking across his palm. It was quite a nice sensation, if a bit odd. And the oddness grew and grew. His fingertips started to sting a little, like getting a paper cut. He pulled his hand away in surprise but the sensation continued to ripple through him, spreading up his arms and over his chest and his scalp like a shiver.

Simon looked back at the animal.

'That was weird, eh, Gubbin … Gubbin … huh,' said Simon as the tingle slowly faded and his head cleared. 'You know, that sounds … perfect. If you were my pet, I'd call you Gubbin.'

The not-quite-a-monkey thing wagged its tail. It didn't look scared any more.

'You like that? You like the sound of Gubbin?'

The creature grinned and sat down, its eyes bright and gleaming as it waited for Simon to say or do something else. And that was the strangest part of it. Simon, try

as he might, usually couldn't get a trained dog to sit, and he'd had the time to practise as he lived next door to a lot of dogs. But here was this creature, unknown until a moment ago, and it was sitting and peacefully watching him. It had been scared but now it looked happy. It almost seemed to be waiting for Simon to speak. It wanted to listen.

And Simon found himself wanting to tell it a story.

His mind began to whir – he swore he could almost hear it. He soon realised his mistake. Three of the security cameras attached to the castle gates had come to life. They were whirring as they turned to face him, their lenses spinning slowly to focus on the creature and him.

Simon gave a silly smile and a small wave to the cameras. It seemed like the polite thing to do. He stared at his waving hand. The shivering sensation had vanished. What was that all about?

Then he remembered his comic. He was making himself later by the second! Simon waved goodbye to the strange animal.

'Sorry, Gubbin, no time for stories! But I'll see you again soon. Enjoy life in the castle.'

Simon disappeared around the corner.

The animal now known as Gubbin turned and stared up the drive at the towering castle of stone. As it watched, something huge and dark slunk out from behind the manicured bushes that lined the easterly castle wall. It started to pad towards Gubbin, picking up speed as it first loped, then galloped, then leaped over the little

cowering animal's head and the high bars of the gates in a single bound. It ran off in the same direction as Simon.

Gubbin gazed through the bars at the disappearing beast. It could still feel the presence of Simon's hand on its head. His touch had been magnetic. It would have followed him anywhere, for the boy had known his real name. Only a Teller had such a power. But they were all long gone . . .

And now The Shadow was on the hunt,

which meant it must also have sensed his power. Which probably meant the end of the boy.

Up on the fourth floor of Castle Fearless, far from Simon, far from Gubbin, far from the beast, a curtain twitched once more as an old hand slowly pulled it closed.

A croaky voice muttered in the half-light. 'He touched it . . . and lived. Remarkable.'

A long sigh.

'But he won't survive the day. Oh, what have we done? Will this madness never end?'

Far from that mystery, Simon ran and ran, the wind whipping past him. His mind had returned to the task at hand, and he only slowed when he reached the main cross-roads into town.

To his left there was a small crooked path that led down, through great thickets of bramble, to the bank of the town's lake. Simon could take the path, run around the edge of the lake and cut twenty minutes off his journey. That way he would definitely reach the comic shop in time.

But it was never going to happen. To go that way he'd have to pass beneath Turnaway Bridge. Which was impossible. He just couldn't do it, even in broad daylight. It was an old fear, a raw fear, one of those rules you just obey. Like not stepping on the cracks in the pavement, or not going into the woods at night, or avoiding those parts of a map which carry the warning, 'Here Be Monsters'.

As far back as Simon could remember he'd always been scared of Turnaway Bridge. He couldn't even explain it to himself, but there was something about the place that made goosebumps crawl across his flesh. He'd never even got close enough for a proper look, and never failed to shut his eyes when his family drove over it in the car.

Simon's mum always said it was his overactive imagination playing tricks on him. Perhaps she was right, but Simon decided, once again, that conquering this particular fear could wait for another day, or week, or year, and he sprinted away to the right.

As he ran he felt a tickle on the back of his neck. He had the strangest feeling that he was being watched. Simon glanced over his shoulder, but there was nothing there. He shook his head. It must be his mind

toying with him, muddling up thoughts of little Gubbin, and the twitching curtain in the window of the castle.

He laughed to shake off the feeling, and ran on.

But unknown to Simon, something *was* watching him, and this time it was not a sweet little animal tucked away behind bars. A fierce snort erupted from the brambles by the path. It was a wet, thick, horrible noise that rose from The Shadow crouched in the undergrowth.

It was a genuinely freaky sound . . . and it was only the beginning.

CHAPTER 3

TELLING TALL TALES

He was never going to make it! Simon had run and run until his heart was beating so hard he thought it might burst out of his chest and race off into the distance on its own, but he still wasn't there. He had to keep running, so he shut his eyes and concentrated on trying to breathe while his feet pounded the pavement. He was close, so close to his goal that he could almost feel the crisp comic pages between his fingers . . . but just thinking about it reminded him of the sensation of stroking the strange fur on Gubbin's head.

Unfortunately, shutting his eyes proved to be a very bad idea. The next thing Simon felt was a huge slap of pain as he ran straight into the back of a bus that someone seemed to have carelessly parked in the middle of the pavement.

Simon sat up in a daze. As his vision cleared he realised his first impression had been incorrect. He hadn't run into a bus – he'd run into Luke Gristle. This was an easy mistake to make, however, as Luke was in the year above Simon, played a LOT of rugby and was really, really strong.

'Watch out,' said Luke, twisting his giant neck to see what sort of blind fool had run into him. 'Oh, hello, Simon. Why did you run into me, you blind fool?'

Simon stared past Luke. His mouth dropped open.

'Is this . . . the END of the queue?'

'Yup,' said Luke with a frown. 'I don't think we'll be getting our comics today.'

Luke was right to be worried. There were a lot of children ahead of them and they were all there for the same reason: to get their hands on a comic. But not necessarily the same comic, for it wasn't just **FEARLESS** fans in the queue. In Simon's opinion **FEARLESS** was clearly the best comic in the world, but there was a challenger, another comic to compete with **FEARLESS**. It was called **FREAKY** and it came out on the same day. No one knew where **FREAKY** was made, and perhaps it was better NOT to know because **FREAKY** was a comic filled with unending weirdness and gore. Lots of gore. And scares. It

was probably drawn in a graveyard.

Every child in town had their personal favourite. You were either a **FEARLESS** Fanatic or a **FREAKY** Fiend. Simon was proud to be a Fanatic even if, unlike his little sister Ruby, he never really felt particularly fearless himself.

Missing out on a copy of either was unthinkable, but it was a very real danger. The creators of both comics had realised long ago that if they printed a limited number of comics – in other words, not enough for every fan to get one – every week would become a major, sell-out event. Children all over the country would struggle to get their hands on the latest adventure. You had to be there each and every Saturday morning if you wanted to be in with a chance.

Simon had always arrived early. He'd seen some large queues for the latest issues of **FEARLESS** and **FREAKY** but from much, much further up the line. This was just ridiculous. The line in front of him led round and round and round the block, before finally arriving at the shop.

Time for action, thought Simon, cracking his knuckles in preparation. He might not have been the bravest boy in the world but the one thing Simon knew he was good at was telling tall tales. He had always found it easy to conjure bizarre and imaginative stories with ease, using his surroundings or

simple props for inspiration. It was just the way his mind had always worked. As skills went, Simon didn't think it was all that remarkable, but it certainly had its uses.

Staring at the queue, Simon plunged his hands into the deep pockets of his shorts and began to rummage. He hoped he was carrying enough knick-knacks to keep the stories alive.

'Er, Luke,' asked Simon, 'have I ever told you the tale of the mythical Fisticuff Foes Collector Card?'

Simon pulled a card from his pocket and waved it under Luke's nose. It showed a picture of a giant robotic monster wearing a top hat and a cape. Luke studied the card with a raised eyebrow.

'Mythical? Right. What makes it so special?'

Simon could tell he had Luke's attention and stepped quickly past him, the playing card dancing through his fingers as he moved.

'Well,' Simon continued, 'this Lord Smackdown card was once owned by a great sorcerer named Wilhelm the Wealthy.' He flourished the card again, with a twinkle in his eye. 'It was said that whoever owned the card would become rich beyond their wildest dreams.'

Luke's eyes glazed over and his mouth hung slack. Simon frowned. It was one thing to get kids to listen to him, but this was extreme.

'Rich?' Luke slurred. Clearly the thought of piles of loot was enough to send him into a trance.

Simon nodded.

'Yes, yes, rich . . . and brilliant at sports. Here you go,' said Simon with an innocent grin, and he flicked the card into Luke's open mouth. *One down*, he thought, *lots to go.*

Simon turned to face Abigail Bitterlip (**FREAKY** Fiend), the smartest girl at school and the next in line. Abigail was very clever but she was also absent-minded, misplacing an average of seven pens a day – one black, three blue, two green and one red.

'Are you telling silly stories again, Simon?' she asked, with her arms folded.

'Silly? No,' said Simon with a smile. 'Stories? Well, yes.'

And Simon proceeded to captivate Abigail, and solve her problems, with a single pen that could write in black, blue, red or green, changing colour with a simple twist of the lid. A pen which, according to Simon, had last been used by the King of Buldavia to write an epic love poem to his sweetheart Esmeralda while she was imprisoned in the Fortress of Brooding Torment, deep in the heart of the Thorny Forest. Best of all, the pen was attached to a rubber band so Abigail could tie it to her wrist. It was, in Simon's words, 'unloseable'.

Although he wondered whether he'd gone overboard with that particular story, Abigail's wide eyes and even wider smile told their own tale. Just like Luke, she'd

been entranced by Simon's imagination and gift of the gab. Simon grinned as he moved up the queue again. Maybe he had become a better storyteller than he'd given himself credit for.

As he approached each boy or girl in the queue, Simon would rustle up a taller and taller tale, each time surprising himself at the speed with which the children fell under his spell. His shrinking pocket supplies were providing all the ideas and bargaining power he needed.

Jermaine Flannel (**FEARLESS** Fanatic) happily made way in exchange for a single shiny bolt — a bolt that had been used to

hold the American flag in place on the moon, during the first lunar landing, supposedly; while Simon's gift of a never-ending gobstopper – found in the heart of a volcano on the mystical Isla de Monstera – worked like magic on Emma Skettle (**FREAKY** Fiend.)

Even grumpy Ben Chub (**FEARLESS** Fanatic), who had absolutely no intention of letting Simon pass, sat down with a happy smile after being presented with a double-ended yo-yo … a double-ended yo-yo that had apparently been used by David to bash Goliath!

Simon scratched his head. He was making progress but it was taking too long.

There were still so many children ahead of him! Simon needed to bring out the big guns. Although he hated talking in front of a crowd he would have to dazzle the mob. It was the only way forwards.

Jumping on top of a rubbish bin, Simon shut his eyes – partly to block out the sea of faces in front of him and partly in concentration. The fear of speaking to so many people all at once began to rise in his stomach. He dug to the very bottom of his right-hand pocket.

'Attention, friends! Gather round, for I have a tale for YOU! The tale to end all tales! The tale of the . . .'

But as the children turned to face him, Simon found his fingers raking through thin air. Had his deep pockets finally run dry? No . . . there . . . in the deepest recess, beneath his pocket money, was a small squishy packet.

He gripped the mysterious object tightly and triumphantly pulled it free.

'This is the tale of the . . . packet of novelty balloons.'

Laughter erupted from the queue. Simon looked at what he was holding. It genuinely was a bag of novelty-shaped balloons. There were penguins and pigs and sumo wrestlers on the packaging. The laughter rose around him like a tide,

threatening to wash him off his perch.

Simon's storytelling spell had been broken. The last of his confidence vanished in a second. He was now just a boy standing on a rubbish bin, holding a packet of balloons and feeling extremely silly.

'Go on, Simon. Tell us a tale about a balloon.'

'Yeah. You're full of hot air, so this should be easy!'

The giggles grew stronger and Simon felt his cheeks reddening. His fears were threatening to take over – to swallow him whole. He stuffed the balloons back in his pocket and glanced around, desperately searching for inspiration. From his raised position he could see clearly across the garden walls of the nearest houses, across the gardens and into the kitchens, into the normal everyday lives of everybody in this normal everyday neighbourhood. Nothing was out of place. Everything was completely and totally unremarkable.

Except for the huge dark shadow which loomed in the nearest garden.

A cold feeling gnawed at Simon's insides. The shadow was crouching low, in the middle of a vegetable patch, facing Simon. Staring at him. No one else was even aware of how close they were to the beast.

Fear began to swell up like a rising tide in Simon's stomach. He jumped up and down on the rubbish bin and waved his arms frantically, shouting at the top of his lungs, not caring how stupid he looked.

'Beat it, foul beast! Get out of here!'

The shadow squatted, frozen, just for a second. Then the great dark mass flicked across the grass, disappearing from view behind a washing line.

All that remained was Simon's adrenalin, and his imagination, each competing for attention. Oh, and the tingle. The fluttering, tingling sensation left by Gubbin's touch had returned. It was pulling at him, inspiring a story in the corner of his mind.

First there had been the curtain twitching at the castle window, then the feeling of being watched at the crossroads . . . and now this. Was the shadow real or was Simon seeing things that weren't there? Had there really been something in that garden? It could have been a trick of the light. A disorientating smudge of darkness, and nothing more.

Simon felt charged. His imagination strained to fill in the blank space and then suddenly, without warning, his lips began to move and words flowed out with curious ease. The voice that left Simon's mouth sounded different to him. It was confident in a way he'd never quite felt. Simon let the words come, the sentences falling easily into place as his mind focused on the shadow...

' . . . The Shadow was an unnatural thing. It was a glimpse of an unknown species. Something from another world, a world so close to Earth, separated by the thinnest margin, a gap no wider than a sheet of paper. And through a great stitched doorway that smelled of old leather, The Shadow had arrived, drawn to our world by the promise of freedom, the promise of a better life. Unfortunately for humankind, someone had long since twisted The Shadow's mind, setting it on a dangerous path. It now lived only for the hunt. And the hunt was on . . . The hunt was him . . . He was the hunt . . .'

The words dried up as quickly as they had begun.

Simon closed his mouth and became aware of the noise. Or rather, the lack of it. He was surrounded by an almost deafening silence: it was the sound of an awful lot of people listening really, really hard. He looked down and his gaze was met by a sea of staring faces. Every child was watching him. No one was laughing now.

A hand was raised near the front of the crowd. It belonged to Joey Chen (**FREAKY** Fiend).

'What . . . what was The Shadow?' asked Joey.

Simon paused. His audience didn't realise he'd really seen something in the garden. They thought he'd been making it all up as he went along. Just Simon being Simon, telling another of his tall tales.

Well, waste not want not, thought Simon, as he dropped to the pavement and slowly strolled up the queue towards the front. Every face tracked him, waiting for an answer. Simon was a little unnerved by all the attention. The only person Simon had ever seen looking completely spellbound by his stories was Ruby, which Simon put down to the fact that she was four years old.

Oh, and Gubbin.

Simon realised he had to say something. Anything.

'Um, The Shadow was . . . a child-stealing beast,' said Simon, enjoying the excited looks of the crowd. 'A horrendous monster, er . . . bred for a single purpose . . . To kidnap kids!'

Simon was so distracted by his enthralled audience that he almost jumped out of his skin when a large hand clamped down on his shoulder, holding him in a vice-like grip.

He turned slowly and came face to face with the Captain.

CHAPTER 4

CAPTAIN ARMSTRONG

'Ar, that be a dark tale for such a nice lad to tell,' said the Captain, raising one thick black eyebrow at Simon. 'My kind of tale, actually.'

Simon looked around. He couldn't believe his eyes. He'd done it! His story-telling had helped him worm his way to the very front of the queue, a feat no one had ever achieved.

Like every previous Saturday, Captain Armstrong was proudly guarding the entrance to The Shipshape Shop. And the doors were still closed. The shop wasn't even open yet. Simon would definitely be able to get this week's issue of **FEARLESS**!

Simon stared up at the Captain. The Captain stared back. He was well known for his love of staring contests. Simon blinked first, which was unsurprising as the Captain had a gnarly old face and a mean stare – a stare he had apparently learned during his legendary duel with the Hurtle-Hate Behemoth.

If there was anyone in town who had as many tales to tell as Simon, it was the Captain. The difference between their stories was that the Captain claimed that his were based on real-life adventures. But as Captain Armstrong's stories all took place on a galleon, featuring pirates and monsters and cutlasses and great big sea battles, Simon found it hard to believe they could be true. Especially the one in which he claimed to have won his Shipshape Shop in a bet with a talking monkey and a crime-busting vending machine.

But the truth didn't matter to Simon when the stories were so fantastic and exciting. He thought the Captain's stories were even more remarkable than the man's appearance, which was saying something. Captain Armstrong was dressed, as ever, in the immaculate uniform of an eighteenth-century Royal Naval officer complete with bicorn hat. The morning sun reflected off the gold buttons on his spotless blue jacket, his starched white breeches shone brightly, and his highly polished black buckle shoe glistened. Captain Armstrong was an impressive sight.

'Brave wayfarers and 'eroes of the 'igh comic seas,' he bellowed, in a voice that rumbled like thirty-foot waves on a stormy night, 'there be treasures to share and not a second to spare – so ENTER . . . if ye dare!'

Captain Armstrong rattled a huge set of brass keys, unlocked the doors and threw them wide open. His booming voice had finally broken the spell Simon had cast on the other children. They surged forwards in their desperation to get inside.

As Simon followed him in, the Captain gave him another hard look.

'Ye 'as a real way with words, lad.'

'Thanks,' said Simon. And because it's polite to return a compliment, he added, 'You too.'

Captain Armstrong laughed, but to Simon it was more of a roar.

'All I be tellin' is memories. Makin' up

stories is a gift. Ye parents must be proud.'

Simon nodded.

'Yeah, I guess. My dad likes my stories. He loves comics too.'

'Well, ye be in good company. Never trust a grown-up who's forgotten 'ow to take pleasure in youthful pursuits.'

The Captain winked and clomped off, his wooden leg thumping against the floorboards.

'I mean, just ye take a look at my shop, lad,' he shouted. 'I never grew up, and I don't plan on startin' now!'

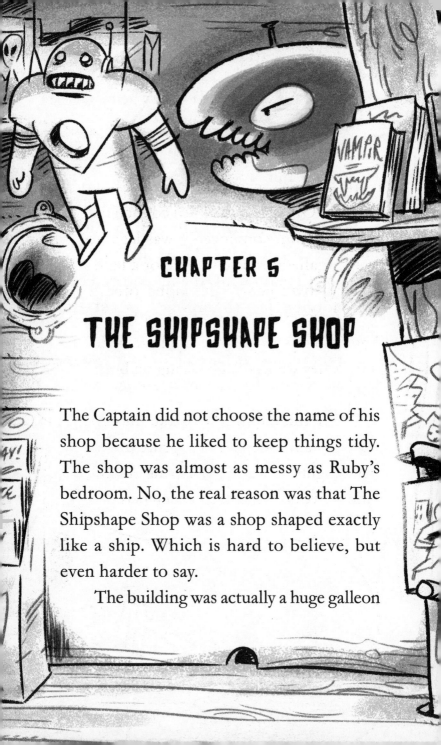

CHAPTER 5

THE SHIPSHAPE SHOP

The Captain did not choose the name of his shop because he liked to keep things tidy. The shop was almost as messy as Ruby's bedroom. No, the real reason was that The Shipshape Shop was a shop shaped exactly like a ship. Which is hard to believe, but even harder to say.

The building was actually a huge galleon

complete with masts and barnacles and cannon. Originally the local council had been far from convinced it was legal to park a galleon in the middle of a land-locked town centre, let alone turn it into a successful shop which only sold the kind of stuff a child would want to buy. They were proved wrong on both counts.

For the children of Lake Shore, the Captain's shop was a treasure trove of delights. It was like entering Aladdin's cave . . . only much, much better.

Books, drawing supplies, toys, computer games, radio-controlled cars, models and countless other spellbinding treats lined the aisles, nooks and crannies of The Shipshape Shop's interior. Kites, telescopes, dolls and inflatable beach loungers in the shape of killer crabs hung from the ceiling. One corner was entirely devoted to a sweet shop famous for supplying more flavours of sugared popping candy than was sensible – garlic, Marmite and bellybutton fluff to name but three.

But every Saturday morning the mountains of goodies and treats filling the Captain's shop seemed to fade into the background. All that mattered on Saturdays were the comics. Every boy and girl felt the same. Simon couldn't keep the grin from his face as he approached the battered wooden counter behind which Captain Armstrong now stood.

'Not that I need to guess, but what'll it be, lad?' said the Captain.

'One **FEARLESS**, please,' said Simon.

Captain Armstrong turned to a shelf behind the counter which was heaving with copies of the comic. Plucking one from the top he handed it to Simon with a smile.

FEARLESS, Issue 2287. Against all the odds, Simon had managed the impossible and secured his prize. He gazed at the cover in delight. It featured a small adventurer standing on top of a huge pile of dazed warriors. She was tiny in comparison to both the pile and the huge battle axe she was clutching. Her red hair almost looked like it was on fire. Simon grinned. *Red's Revenge* was one of Simon's favourite stories.

'Thanks, Captain. See you next week,' said Simon, and he placed his money on the counter and turned to leave.

'Ar, not so fast, lad. "Aven't ye forgotten somethin'?'

The Captain pointed to his left. There, propped up against the wall, was a coffin. An actual coffin. The lid was propped open and inside it was a large stack of black envelopes. Simon walked over to the coffin and picked up the top envelope. The envelopes were simply labelled **FREAKY**, with a small warning that read, *Your nightmares begin NOW, Kids!* The words looked like they had been written with dripping blood.

'Ye best friend wouldn't be too 'appy if ye forgot to take 'IS treasure 'ome . . . would 'e?'

'No, he wouldn't – thanks,' said Simon. Simon had been picking up both his comic and Whippet's every week for the past two years. His friend wasn't keen on crowds or the outside world, and Simon was more than happy to do him this small favour. He dropped the extra money for Whippet's comic on the counter, gripped his purchases and waved farewell. Much to Simon's surprise, Captain Armstrong gave him a sharp salute.

'Best of luck, lad,' he said. 'I 'ope you

an' young Whippet know 'ow to swim, because there's a real storm comin'.'

Simon frowned at the Captain. What an odd thing to say on such a sunny day. He pushed on, wiggling through the crowd. He had to force his way past all the shoulders and arms and bags and rucksacks, including one child with a particularly huge backpack – a pack so big that he couldn't

even see who was carrying it.

Captain Armstrong watched Simon leave before slowly pulling a well-read copy of last week's **FEARLESS** from inside his jacket. He dropped the comic on the counter, where it fell open instantly at the *Batty Beasts* strip. The Captain had meant what he'd said. A storm was coming, and it wouldn't be water that the boys would soon find themselves wading through, but something much more icky.

He snarled into his beard, wishing he could help them. But Captain Armstrong had rules to obey.

There were always rules. But his time to play a part would come soon enough.

No one could keep an old sea dog down for ever.

CHAPTER 6

A CANINE CATASTROPHE

As Simon walked slowly back up Stapleton Drive, he decided his babysitting duties could wait for five more minutes. He had a much more important task to complete first.

Stopping outside his neighbours' house, the bright blue door of number 42, Simon experienced the same strange warning tickle spreading across the back of his neck. *Not again,* he thought. He'd had quite enough false alarms for one morning. The walk home had given him time to think and he'd begun to wonder if he'd seen anything strange at all in that garden.

Perhaps the big shadow had just been . . . a shadow.

Only a fool was fooled by foolish things. His mum had said that once, when Simon and his dad had tried to convince her the Loch Ness Monster might be real. Simon's mum never believed in anything weird or strange – and there were *photos* of the Loch Ness Monster. Simon's imagination, however, was so vivid that he sometimes had trouble separating genuine fact from fiction . . . especially when the fiction was so interesting.

As Simon stood on the doorstep of the

house with the bright blue door, a wild and giant smear of black appeared behind him. The Shadow was alive. It had bounded from garden to alley to bush to tree as it tracked Simon home, moving with an unnatural speed. The Shadow was an unnatural size too. An unnatural shape. And perhaps strangest of all, it seemed to be clutching half a gnome in its mouth.

Simon spun on his heel. But there was nothing to see. He shook himself. He really had to stop jumping at shadows.

Turning back, he reached up, gripped his neighbours' brass door knocker – which was shaped like a St. Bernard dog carrying a rubber ring in its mouth – and brought it down with a great thump.

But the door was already open.

As it swung slowly inwards Simon heard the start of a low rumble. The rumble grew into a roar. The roar became a cacophony of wild sounds that rattled the windows and shook tiles from the roof. It sounded to Simon's imaginative mind like a pack of foul hellish beasts dragged back to life from beyond the grave.

And through the open doorway he saw them.

Bounding towards him in a rolling mound of slathering jaws, spittle and moulting hair was an avalanche of dogs.

Pooches and hounds of every size, shape and colour were hurtling headlong through the house. The hounds slammed into his legs, picked Simon up and deposited him on the pavement. But instead of eating him alive, the canine horde simply licked him happily from head to toe. Unable to struggle his way to freedom, Simon collapsed in a fit of giggles under the tickling effect of their bright pink tongues.

Simon began to fear he might actually die of laughter, until a strong hand gripped him by the shirt front and hauled him clear of the wagging mass.

Simon gazed up into the round friendly face of Mrs Willow, his best friend's mum, and professional dog sitter for the entire neighbourhood.

'How many times have I told you – DON'T USE THE

KNOCKER! It drives this lot doolally!'

'Sorry, Mrs Willow, my head's been all over the place today,' said Simon.

Mrs Willow laughed and headed through the house towards the kitchen, closely followed by the slobbering dog pack.

'Well, it's always nice to see you, Simon. Comic day, is it?'

'Er, yeah,' said Simon. 'Is Whippet in?'

'Of course he's in, dear. He's ALWAYS in,' said Mrs Willow as she poured dog food into a dozen bowls. 'You're about the only reason he ever leaves that cave of his. I sometimes worry about the boy . . .'

'No need to worry today, Mrs Willow. It's treehouse weather,' Simon said as he headed upstairs. 'I'll have him outdoors in no time.'

But as Simon was about to discover, nothing is ever that simple.

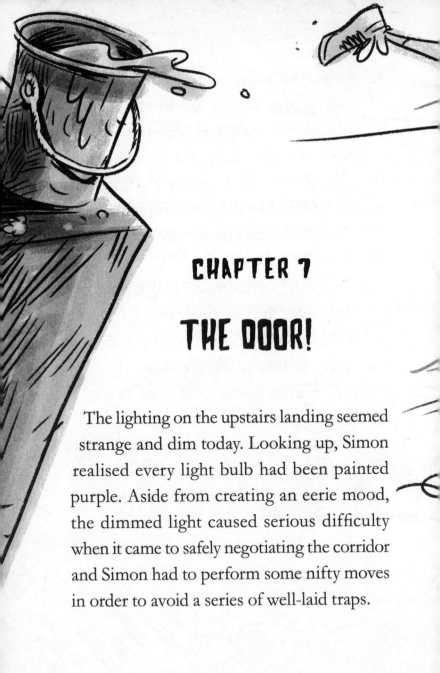

CHAPTER 7

THE DOOR!

The lighting on the upstairs landing seemed strange and dim today. Looking up, Simon realised every light bulb had been painted purple. Aside from creating an eerie mood, the dimmed light caused serious difficulty when it came to safely negotiating the corridor and Simon had to perform some nifty moves in order to avoid a series of well-laid traps.

A tripwire had been rigged to a bucket of dirty water balanced on a high shelf. He hopped over the wire and quickly curled into a forward roll in order to avoid a giant sheet of sticky see-through flypaper that was hanging from the ceiling.

Cunning, thought Simon, *but not cunning enough*. Now all he had to do was open the door ...

NOPE!

KEEP
OUT

Standing before him was a gateway to another world. An extremely freaky-looking world. The door was painted solid black but it was almost entirely obscured by the hundreds of signs, notices, warnings and hexes covering the surface.

'Keep Out' . . . 'Buzz Off' . . . 'Get Lost' . . . 'All Who Enter Be Cursed' . . .

The door was illuminated by two flaming torches (battery powered, but very realistic) and there were enough voodoo dolls, skulls, emblems and other horrible trinkets to ward off an entire army of evil intruders. A devil-shaped mask hung from a string seemed to come alive in the flickering light, its mouth opening wide and cackling.

PLZ, GO
AWAY

Simon's voice caught in his throat. This was the moment of truth. He leaned close to the woodwork, drew a deep breath and shouted, 'Hey, it's me – Simon. Open up, you weirdo!'

Locks clicked, gears meshed and turned, bolts slid back and finally the bedroom door opened wide enough for a small mirror on a stick to pop through the gap. It was the sort of device Simon's favourite comic heroes might use to check for approaching enemies. The mirror turned quickly, left and right, paused to study Simon, then disappeared back into the gloom.

The door sprung open, two hands grabbed Simon by the shoulders and he was hauled across the threshold.

Behind him, the door slammed shut again, and Simon's best friend in the whole world, Whippet Willow, scurried to his desk and slumped into a battered swivel chair. He scowled in concentration, picked up a pencil and without even a 'hello', he returned to his drawing.

It was an odd greeting but Simon was used to his friend's strange ways. Sitting in his chair, his head bent over his work, Whippet was wearing, as ever, his favourite green plastic visor, pulled low over his eyes. According to Whippet it kept his spiky black hair from

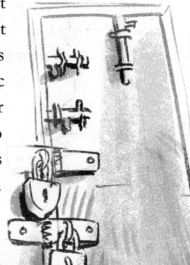

falling in his face but Simon knew he actually wore it because he thought it looked cool, and different. Like his beloved black T-shirt emblazoned with a picture of a skull.

Whippet was a little freaky.

'What's with the extra security?' asked Simon, studying the twelve new locks on Whippet's door.

Whippet leaned back, sharpened his pencil and gave the skylight above his desk a wary look.

'Firstly, I've seen something really weird prowling around outside. Could just be a cat, but if it is, it's a really BIG cat. All I can make out is its shadow, and that's bad enough.'

Simon's mouth fell open. Whippet was famously known for distrusting absolutely everything. He could find a conspiracy inside a packet of crisps. But today Whippet was talking about seeing shadows – this must be more than a coincidence. Simon swallowed as he remembered the strange incident in the queue. Had he and Whippet seen the same shadow? He was dying to ask him all about it but decided to keep quiet for now. There was no way Whippet would ever agree to leave his bedroom if he thought there was some strange monster lurking in the bushes, and Simon really needed his friend by his side.

'Secondly,' Whippet continued, 'we had old Mrs Brandon's Chihuahua staying here last week and the little flea-factory managed to get in my room. She ate six erasers, drank a bottle of ink and peed all over the place. It was such a mess I had to stop drawing for a whole hour!'

Which was actually quite a big deal. Whippet Willow had a special skill, his one true passion: he was extremely good at drawing – particularly comics. As Whippet liked to tell his and Simon's classmates, he first discovered his talent when, at the age of six, he swallowed a pencil. According to the legend of Whippet, told by Whippet, from that day forth he was connected to his drawings 'at a molecular level'.

The truth however, was that after the surgeons had removed the pencil from Whippet's stomach, he had been stuck in the children's hospital for two weeks with nothing to do but read piles and piles of old issues of **FREAKY**. He reread the comics so many times he knew them all by heart, and one day, feeling bored, he picked up another pencil and, instead of eating it, began to scribble drawings from his favourite comic stories . . . from memory.

And the pictures

were perfect.

'All done,' said Whippet, holding up a drawing of an armoured whale on wheels being driven by a pack of zombified giraffes.

'Haha – brilliant,' said Simon, impressed as always by his friend's talent, 'but drop your pencils. We're heading next door. I've got to look after Ruby this afternoon and you're helping.'

'Nah, sorry, no can do,' said Whippet, spinning slowly in his chair. 'The real world and me, we just don't get along.'

'You do realise that this is our last summer together? The last one before everything changes?'

Whippet nodded

as he took his sketchbook back from Simon and opened it to a fresh page. The end of the holiday would bring with it new schools for both boys. They were growing up, moving on and moving apart. Whippet had been offered a full scholarship to a private school just out of town that specialised in the arts, while Simon was heading to the local school, Lake Shore Academy. Neither had spoken much about it since Whippet had received his acceptance letter. It felt almost like a ticking time-bomb for their friendship. Not talking about it had been the simplest and best solution.

'I don't know what's going to happen next year, but right now we don't have a second to spare. There's an adventure outside with your name on it,' said Simon.

'Looking after Ruby is not an adventure.'

Whippet had started drawing again. Simon had to move fast.

'I wasn't talking about Ruby,' he said.

'Then what?' said Whippet, looking up from his work, his curiosity getting the better of him.

'You'll never find out unless you follow me,' said Simon, revealing the envelope containing Whippet's copy of **FREAKY**. Simon began to back towards the door, waggling the comic as he went.

'Hey, wait! No fair! Gimme! That's cheating!' said Whippet, chasing after Simon.

Occasionally you have to be cruel to be kind, thought Simon, as the two boys sprinted downstairs and out into the sunshine . . .

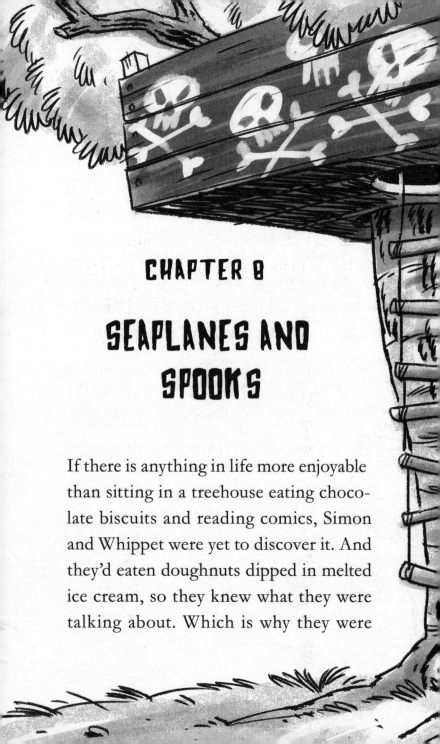

CHAPTER 8

SEAPLANES AND SPOOKS

If there is anything in life more enjoyable than sitting in a treehouse eating chocolate biscuits and reading comics, Simon and Whippet were yet to discover it. And they'd eaten doughnuts dipped in melted ice cream, so they knew what they were talking about. Which is why they were

planning to spend the rest of the afternoon hiding from the world inside their own secret leafy lair. Simon also hoped the treehouse would make a useful vantage point for spotting shadowy creatures. Not that Simon really believed in monsters, but he felt you could never be too careful.

The treehouse in question was built in the branches of the old apple tree at the bottom of Simon's garden. Simon wasn't very good at woodwork and the camp had begun life as three planks of wood nailed together one metre above the lawn. Thankfully his dad had offered his assistance. Since then they'd made a LOT of improvements. They'd raised the base and extended it with extra walkways, outposts and flags. Even Ruby had offered a helping hand by scribbling on the wood with her crayons, drawing what looked to Simon like a simple skull and crossbones. Whippet thought it looked pretty good and had brought down a big box of paints and set about creating a huge mural which had considerably more skulls and bones than were necessary.

But it looked cool.

As a finishing touch Simon had dragged a couple of old beanbags into the treehouse, to use as chairs. It was as fine a camp as any eleven year old could wish for.

While Ruby played with a herd of cuddly toy dinosaurs on the grass below, Simon and Whippet lay in their camp, flicking through their new comics.

Babysitting really wasn't that bad a chore when your sister was happy entertaining herself, and Ruby was easily pleased.

So was Whippet. Simon's friend had been so engrossed in his comic that he'd barely noticed they were outdoors, far from the safety of his bedroom and the comfort of his drawings. The only thing that had drawn his attention away from his copy of **FREAKY** was Simon recalling his encounter with the strange little creature at the gates of Castle Fearless. Whippet had started asking all sorts of questions about Gubbin's appearance. What were its ears like? What was its fur like? How long was its tail? Simon had done his best to describe the animal and, as he spoke, Whippet had pulled a small sketchbook from his pocket and started scribbling.

But try as he might, Simon simply couldn't answer all of his friend's questions, as he hadn't studied the creature for long enough. Whippet didn't seem to mind. He just popped his sketchbook back in his pocket and the pair returned to their comics.

It was late afternoon when Whippet finally lifted his head from the pages of **FREAKY**.

'Look at this, Mossy. Just look at this,' he said.

Whippet passed Simon his comic. It was open on an episode of *Ghoul School*, a story about a class of undead kids and their ongoing struggle to attend lessons in mummification and devil worship while fending off countless human monster-hunters and foul beasts from the underworld.

Simon grinned and held open his copy of **FEARLESS**.

'Nice. But check out this week's *Knuckles and Duster*.'

Knuckles and Duster was an all-action epic that charted the adventures of a masked man with a mysterious past (Knuckles), who travelled the globe in a converted MV-22 Osprey seaplane known as the 'Silent Kite'.

Together with his pilot, Chuck Duster, Knuckles hunted for the shadowy criminal gang responsible for stealing his memories and his true identity.

Whippet pored over the comic, instantly lost in admiration for the artwork. Simon gazed out from the treehouse. He paused, looked again, then the breath caught in his throat.

He'd seen it.

Only for a moment, but he had definitely seen a silhouette of something, racing down the path beside his house. There was no doubt about it. It was The Shadow, the same shadow. And it was big. Very big in fact, and very dark, like a charcoal smudge on the landscape.

Had Whippet seen it this time as well?

But Whippet was not looking at the garden, he was staring at his friend.

'You okay, Mossy? You look like I did when I found Tricksy sitting in a puddle of pee on my bed.'

'Please tell me you saw that,' said

Simon, unable to keep the excitement from his voice. 'The Shadow. It was huge . . . huge . . . it was huge . . .'

As Simon repeated the word 'huge' over and over again, Whippet gave him a playful punch on the arm.

'Simon, for someone who loves words, you seem to have run out of new ones. What's up?'

Simon didn't know how to answer that particular question. His imagination had taken over, racing to suggest possible explanations. He crawled around the treehouse, scanning the corners of the garden, looking for something, anything, to make sense of the mystery. He kneeled and peered over the edge of the platform.

On the grass below, everything looked normal. Ruby was trying to force her Triceratops toy to eat her Tyrannosaurus rex.

A plant-eater swallowing a meat-eater wasn't exactly how things were done in the dinosaur kingdom, but Ruby didn't know any better.

Nothing else seemed to be out of place. Once again he was looking for the extra-ordinary where it didn't exist. Was he acting this way because of his dad's parting request?

If you see anything peculiar, no matter how silly, write to me.

'Okay, you're starting to freak me out a little,' said Whippet, watching Simon crawl from one corner of the treehouse to the other.

Simon stopped. Now was not the time to spook his only ally . . . but he had to talk to someone. Besides, it wasn't only his dad who'd been cryptic.

'Listen, Whippet. Captain Armstrong

said there was "a storm coming" today. At the time I thought he was just being mysterious for fun or something, but now I'm not so sure.'

Whippet shrugged. 'Mossy, you shouldn't believe anything the Captain says. He's completely bonkers. He once told me he ate an entire octopus because it laughed at his hat.'

Simon scratched his head and tried to organise his thoughts.

'I think he was being serious this time. Remember the shadow you saw through your skylight? Well, I think I've seen it too. In town earlier, and right here, just now. I've a feeling that trouble is heading our way . . . Or that trouble has already found us.'

Whippet turned to his best friend in the whole world. Simon had his full attention. Whippet looked worried and swallowed nervously. Then he delivered the last truly innocent sentence of their lives. Ten words that he and Simon would never forget.

'Trouble? What's the worst that could ever happen around here?'

CHAPTER 9

SEVEN SECONDS IN WHICH THE WORST HAPPENED

No sooner had Whippet uttered that immortal sentence than events took a turn for the scary. And as they unfolded before the boys' transfixed eyes, like a tale from the pages of **FREAKY**, time stuttered and slowed. It was unreal, like staring at a series of comic panels. Simon couldn't tear his gaze away, couldn't move a limb to intervene. He couldn't do anything at all but watch in horror.

00:01 The fence between Whippet's house and Simon's garden exploded. Chunks of wood and splinters flew in all directions.

00:02 An enormous shadowy beast leaped through the dust and debris. It landed in a skid and looked all around, swinging its immense head from side to side. It seemed to be searching for something. Searching desperately.

00:04 The beast cast a quick glance back in the direction of Whippet's home. Then it turned and stared at Ruby. It seemed to nod to itself, and picked the little girl up by her T-shirt, like a lioness gripping her cub by the scruff of the neck, before butting its way through the opposite fence. It sprang into the garden of number 38.

00:05 A small person dressed like an explorer, wearing a huge rucksack, leaped over the remains of the Willows' garden fence.

00:07 The same small person dived through the hole leading to number 38 and disappeared from sight.

As shards of fence and bits of shattered dog bowl rained down on the treehouse, Whippet could think of only one thing to say.

'Did you see how big that thing's NOSE was?'

CHAPTER 10

HUH?!?...

Simon was the first to come to his senses.

Leaping from the platform, he landed in a crouch and ran to the damaged fence. Stretching into the distance where The Shadow, Ruby and the small explorer had headed was a row of destroyed hedges, fences and brick walls, and there, just disappearing from view, was a bounding shadow.

Ruby and the
creature were gone.

'Did you see its
nose, though?' said
Whippet, looking dazed as he
joined Simon by the fence.

Simon couldn't speak. Whippet bent
down and picked up Ruby's Triceratops toy.

'Boy, your mum is going to kill you.'

'Forget about me! What about Ruby?
Where's Ruby?' shouted Simon.

It's at times like these that a boy needs
his parents, but fate was not smiling kindly
on Simon. His father was, well, who knew
where, and his mother had gone shopping
and wouldn't be back till supper. He'd been
left alone and in charge and it had all gone
horribly wrong.

Simon began to hyperventilate – which
means breathing really, really fast and

panicking like crazy – an understandable reaction in the circumstances.

Whippet was standing and gazing into his own back garden. Simon's mind whirled. The dogs . . .

'The thing that just grabbed Ruby . . . Your mum looks after some pretty dangerous breeds . . . Could it have been one of her dogs? Could one of them have escaped?'

'I don't think so, Mossy. Take a look at this,' said Whippet.

Simon followed Whippet's gaze. To his surprise, thirty whimpering dogs – including three very timid Rottweilers, four exceptionally nervous Pitballs and an absolutely terrified Doberman – were desperately trying to hide inside a kennel built for one. Their efforts were not being met with much success. On any other day

the boys would have found the massed furry bundle of noses, tails and paws totally hilarious. But not today.

'Weeeeeeeeeird . . .' said Whippet. 'So what do we do now?'

'Now we find my sister before anything happens to her . . . Well, before anything worse happens to her . . . worse than what's already happened to her!' said Simon.

The boys leaped through the hole leading next door, ducking beneath the remains of the hedge into number 38, chasing after Ruby's kidnapper, an unknown horror . . . and an uncertain fate.

CHAPTER 11

NO PLACE LIKE GNOME

Simon and Whippet followed the chaotic path of garden devastation. The huge creature had smashed headlong through bird tables, greenhouses, garden sheds and ponds alike. It looked to Simon as if a monster-shaped hurricane had torn through Stapleton Drive. In particular it seemed to have hit every compost heap in its path.

Whippet was paying little attention to his immediate surroundings. He was staring upwards, watching the late afternoon sun.

'You know, if I have to be outside, why can't it be night?' he said. 'The daytime is filled with noisy people doing noisy things. It's quieter in the dark. More peaceful. Maybe I was a vampire in a previous life –'

'Ruby's lost out here somewhere and you're talking about vampires?' said Simon, turning round to face him as they ran on.

'Sorry, Mossy, that wasn't cool,' he said. Whippet spotted something just ahead of his friend. 'Hey, what's happened here?'

The boys came to a stop in an immaculate garden lined with colourful flowerbeds and perfectly pruned bushes. A pond shaped like a large teardrop sat in the middle of the lawn. Golden-scaled fish shimmied through its crystal-clear water, chasing shadows of their own.

Everything looked perfect except for a single element. In one corner of the grass stood a small collection of garden gnomes – who appeared to have met with a nasty accident.

'Someone's ripped their noses off,' said Whippet. 'Not something you see every day.'

'What a weird coincidence,' said Simon in surprise. 'My dad told me this morning that I could probably conjure a story from a garden gnome. Not sure what tale these poor things would have to tell.'

'They're telling us we're on the right

path. The damage looks new, like they've only just been attacked,' said Whippet.

He was right. Simon swallowed, stared at the unhappy gathering of noseless gnomes and strained to grasp hold of an idea that was bouncing around his head. Not an idea, actually, more of a memory. Something he'd seen. Shadows. Noses. Noses and shadows. It was right there, drifting at the edge of his mind. If only he could grasp it . . .

But it was gone, flushed from his brain by the surprise of something hard pressing into the small of his back. Both boys froze in shock.

A long shadow stretched across the grass between them and a small, angry voice said, 'If you dumbos want to live until dinner, you'd better raise your hands and reach for the sky!'

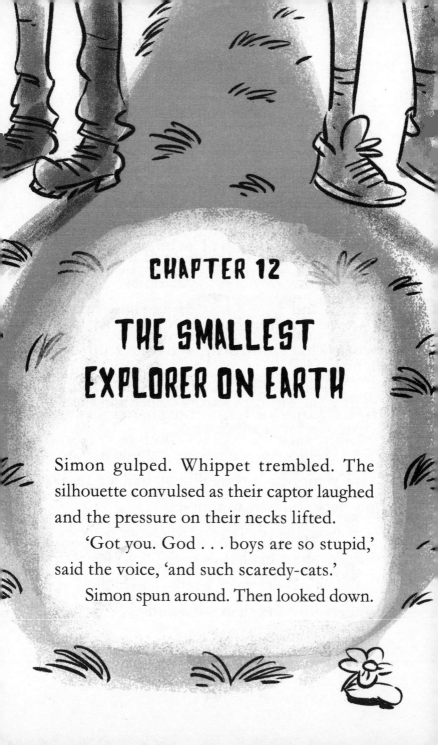

CHAPTER 12

THE SMALLEST EXPLORER ON EARTH

Simon gulped. Whippet trembled. The silhouette convulsed as their captor laughed and the pressure on their necks lifted.

'Got you. God . . . boys are so stupid,' said the voice, 'and such scaredy-cats.'

Simon spun around. Then looked down.

There, scowling at him from beneath the sort of wide white hat he'd seen explorers wearing in history books, was not a shadow, or a bandit, but the same strange character who had run across Simon's garden, chasing the creature that had nabbed Ruby. As explorers went, this one was really a bit on the small side.

She was red-haired and dressed in a worn khaki uniform. Judging from its numerous rips, tears and questionable stains, the uniform and its owner had experienced a lot of adventures.

'You loony – what are you playing at?' said Whippet. 'I thought you had a gun to my back. I nearly wet myself.'

'Couldn't you tell the difference between fingers and a loaded weapon?' said the girl, holding up her empty hands. She folded her fingers into the shape of a gun.

'Well, no, but, um . . .' Whippet began uncertainly. 'That's not the point!'

'If you'd rather I was armed, it can be arranged,' said the girl with a calm smile.

She reached into a huge backpack that was sitting beside her on the grass, and removed two handheld pocket crossbows. The arrows loaded in each bow looked a lot deadlier than a pointed finger.

Simon, summoning a small reserve of courage he didn't know he possessed, decided this was a pretty good moment to intervene.

'Er, look, my name's Simon,' said Simon, holding out his hand, 'and this is my best friend, Whippet.'

The girl looked from one boy to the next. Whippet was staring wide-eyed at the cross-bows. Simon wasn't sure if his friend was terrified or fascinated. Maybe it was a little of both. The girl was watching him as if he was a laboratory experiment that had gone wrong.

When she showed no other sign of reacting, Simon began to feel a bit silly standing and holding out his hand. He gave it a comedy waggle and coughed lightly to get her attention.

'And you are?'

The girl tossed the crossbows back into her bag, and almost reluctantly gave Simon's hand a shake.

'I'm Lucy Shufflebottom, action heroine and explorer extraordinaire,' she said. As the corners of Whippet's mouth began to rise in a predictable smirk, she

added, 'And if you even think about laughing at my surname, I'll chop your knees off.'

While Lucy rearranged the contents of her pack, Whippet clamped both hands over his face to stop even the smallest giggle from escaping – he rather liked his knees and wanted to hold on to them. Simon looked at the girl's massive rucksack.

'Wait a second, didn't I see you earlier? In The Shipshape Shop?' he asked.

'Huh. Very observant. For a boy,' said Lucy.

'Were you buying comics?'

Lucy snorted.

'Comics are almost as stupid as boys. Dangerous too.'

Simon couldn't think of anything to say to that. He turned his attention back to the gnomes.

'Okay, but it was you in my garden earlier? Right? Chasing after that . . . thing? Did it do all this too?' Simon said, pointing to the ornaments.

'Yep,' said Lucy, hoisting her pack on to her back. 'Every gnome, scarecrow, statue or cockerel-shaped weather vane in the beast's path has been de-nosed. It's fascinated with stealing snouts.'

'Like some mental magpie,' said Whippet.

Lucy stopped.

'A magpie? Hmm. You know, it's actually a myth that magpies like to steal things, but the idea is interesting. Very interesting . . .'

Pushing past Simon – her manners left a lot to be desired – Lucy strode towards the gaping hole in the opposite hedge.

'But it's not just about the noses, boys.

I've seen dozens of ransacked kitchens, countless obliterated compost heaps, and every bin across town seems to have been knocked over. That's not magpie behaviour, mythical or otherwise.'

'Where are you going?' asked Simon.

'Why, to hunt it and destroy it, of course. The only reason we're even talking is so I can tell you to stop following me and go home,' replied Lucy.

'Hang on, we weren't following you. That thing's got my little sister.'

Lucy gave Simon a long stare. It wasn't as powerful as Captain Armstrong's, but it was pretty good. It felt like Lucy had been studying the Captain's technique. This time, however, Simon wasn't giving in without a fight. If it cost him his life, he was bringing Ruby home.

'We're not going anywhere until we've rescued her,' he said, summoning all his confidence.

'Okay, fine, if she means so much to you. Personally I'd rather you left this to the professionals. I'm talking about myself, by the way, and I don't need any junior sidekicks.'

Whippet snorted.

'Junior?' he said. 'That's rich. How old are you, anyway?'

'Nine. And if you've a problem with my age, please allow me to reintroduce you to my crossbows.'

'Lucy, we don't care how old you are. We don't want to be your sidekicks and we don't want to get in the way,' said Simon, 'but we have to find Ruby.'

A brief smile flashed across the face of the smallest explorer on Earth.

'Alright. These are the rules. If either of you get eaten, you're on your own. This is one scary beast and aside from your sister, it doesn't take prisoners . . .'

Lucy stepped through the hole in the hedge and gave a final ominous shout.

'. . . and neither, for that matter, do I!'

CHAPTER 13

END OF THE TRAIL

The tornado of destruction and missing noses went on and on, and by six o'clock the trio were growing weary. They'd been trudging for hours, following the winding path of mayhem. Every garden they encountered had been vandalised in the same way. The contents of rubbish bins had been scattered, statues and abandoned toys left outside had been robbed of their noses. Even the occasional kitchen window had been broken. Confused residents, standing and looking at the damage, barely noticed Simon, Lucy and Whippet as they crept from house to house. They stopped to listen as one elderly couple cleared up their mess, bagging the rubbish that had been spread across their lawn.

'Would you look at what those foxes have done, eh, dear?' said the old man, shaking his head in disbelief.

'They get bolder every year,' said the old lady, with a small smile.

Whippet snorted and gestured at the nearby hole in the hedge.

'Foxes? They think all this was caused by foxes? Are they mad?'

Lucy sighed and headed for the next garden.

'No,' she said, climbing over the wreckage. 'They're just adults.'

'What do you mean?' asked Simon.

'Adults make sense of the world by what they already know and can explain. They don't leave much room in their heads for what they don't know. For the unexplainable.'

Whippet nodded enthusiastically.

'You're not wrong. My mum says I'm hard to explain,' he said.

'She sounds like a smart lady,' said Lucy and disappeared through the next gap in the fence before Whippet could respond.

When Simon and Whippet climbed through the remains of the splintered wicker frame, they found Lucy standing on a large patch of scrubland that bordered the lake. In the near distance, in the warm early evening light, Simon could make out the familiar shape of Turnaway Bridge.

He shivered. He'd avoided it once today, and he planned on avoiding it again.

Lucy tilted her head to one side and raised her crossbows in a wary fashion, waving them left and right. She sniffed the breeze and bent down to examine the muddy ground. Whippet sidled up to Simon.

'Are you sure we should be following her, Mossy?' he whispered. 'She's a bit scary.'

'I know, but if she can help us find Ruby, she's the best friend we've got.'

'But wouldn't the police be more use? I mean, look . . . What is she doing?'

Lucy was tracing a pattern through the mud, following the outline of an impression in the dirt. It looked a bit like the outline of a leaf.

'Paw print,' said Lucy, scanning the waste ground. She pointed towards the lake. 'It was heading for the water.'

As Lucy jogged to the water's edge, the boys bent down for a closer inspection. Strange, thought Simon. It didn't look like any print he'd ever seen. It was too perfect, too simplistic. It was exactly what he'd have drawn if he'd been asked to draw a monster footprint. Not that he would have. He left the drawing to the boy with the pencils. And that boy had obviously been thinking the same thing.

'This looks almost fake,' said Whippet, staring at the print. Simon had to agree.

'Yeah . . . it's not from a mammal . . . or a reptile,' said Simon. 'And it's too big to be an amphibian or a bird . . .'

The oddities of the day just kept on piling up, but none of them really mattered. All that counted was finding his sister. She might have been brave, but she was only four years old. It was Ruby's dinner time – even if she wasn't scared she would definitely be getting hungry. Which also meant his mum would be home by now, and that was a whole different sort of problem.

Lucy walked back to the boys with a

scowl on her face. She dropped her bag beside the muddy print and sat down with a thump.

'What is it?' asked Simon. 'What did you find?'

'Nothing,' mumbled Lucy in response.

Simon swallowed.

'You don't mean –' he began.

'Yes. I've lost it. The creature's given me the slip.'

Simon's mouth opened and closed. It had never occurred to him that they might lose the trail. That Ruby might be truly lost. Lucy watched him processing this new information.

'I'm . . . sorry, okay?' she said. 'It must have known we were closing in. It used the water to cover its tracks. Clever critter.'

Whippet bit his lip. 'So what do we do now?' he asked.

'Well, I'm going to sit down here and

think, while you two stay as quiet as mice.'

'How is that going to –' began Whippet, but Lucy held up a hand to silence him.

'Quiet as mice means keeping really quiet. No squeaking, let alone speaking.'

Whippet shook his head and slumped to the ground. He pulled a small pencil and his little sketchbook from the back pocket of his jeans, flipped it open to a new page and started to draw. Simon watched him work. Sketching was a nervous habit of Whippet's and it always seemed to make him feel better.

In fact, it made Simon feel a bit better too. Whippet at work with a pencil in his hand – it was a taste of his normal life, the everyday. Only that morning he'd dreamed of life being more interesting... but not like this. Kidnapped sisters and nose-stealing monsters were not Simon's idea of fun.

And yet he couldn't help but find the situation a tiny bit thrilling. It was pretty exciting in a strange way.

Feeling guilty, he turned from Whippet to look down at Lucy. She was sitting cross-legged, with her forefingers pressed against the sides of her head. Her eyes were shut. Simon had questions that needed answers but Lucy obviously didn't want to share any information with the boys. It was time to try something new. A little detective trickery he'd read about. In the pages of **FEARLESS**, of course.

'Lucy, what are you doing?' he asked.

'Meditating.'

'Is it working?'

'Not yet,' replied Lucy with a growl.

'So are you, like, searching for answers in your inner mind?'

'Something like that, yes.'

'Did it take a long time to get good at it?' asked Simon.

'Years. I started practising when I was three.'

'Wow. Amazing. Did you learn from a book?'

'No, I studied with a Grand Master,' said Lucy.

'That's cool. So what were you doing in The Shipshape Shop?'

'I was there to ask Captain Armstrong's advice on catching this monst— Oh.'

Whippet stopped sketching and turned to Lucy, who was now slapping herself in the forehead and groaning. Simon clapped his hands together and smiled in delight.

'I cannot believe I fell for that,' said

Lucy, lying back, thumping the ground and kicking her legs in annoyance. 'The Question Avalanche method. Oldest trick in the book.'

Simon kicked the sole of Lucy's shoe.

'See, we boys aren't stupid all the time. Now start talking, Lucy. You know more than you're sharing.'

Lucy sighed but continued staring up at the stars, which had begun to emerge in the early evening sky.

'I'm not under any obligation to share

anything with either of you. But if you must know, I've been tracking this monster since last Saturday.'

'What?' said Whippet in surprise. 'A whole week? This beast has been out there, in our town, running loose for a week? How? Where did it come from?'

Lucy puffed out her cheeks. She stayed like that for a while. Silent. Thinking. She seemed to come to a decision.

'Listen, I've got my theories, lots of them, but no real proof. I've seen plenty of things that would turn your hair white and I can tell you for a fact they're not from around here. Not from Earth.'

Whippet's eyes widened in disbelief.

'Are you talking about aliens?'

'Hmm . . . not the right word, but it's

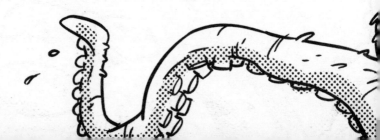

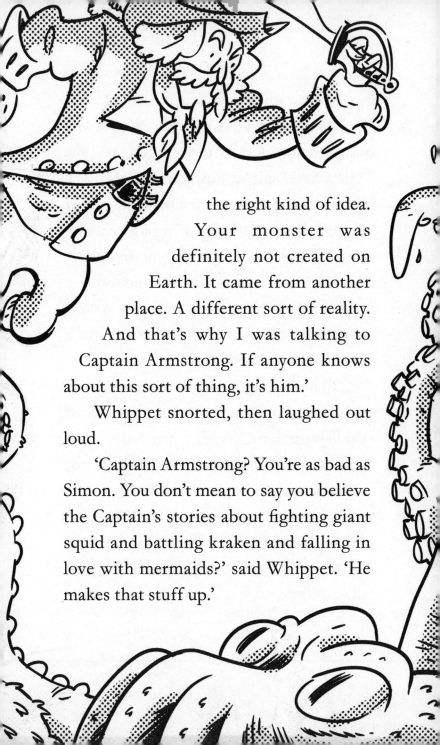

the right kind of idea. Your monster was definitely not created on Earth. It came from another place. A different sort of reality. And that's why I was talking to Captain Armstrong. If anyone knows about this sort of thing, it's him.'

Whippet snorted, then laughed out loud.

'Captain Armstrong? You're as bad as Simon. You don't mean to say you believe the Captain's stories about fighting giant squid and battling kraken and falling in love with mermaids?' said Whippet. 'He makes that stuff up.'

Simon raised a finger.

'Hey, I didn't say his stories were true, but no one has ever proved they're false. They might be true. Anything *could* be true. Ghosts, bogeymen, even aliens. Anything.'

Whippet frowned.

'Okay, but if something's this dangerous or scary, how can anyone ever find out if it's real? If everyone's too scared to get close, how would anyone ever know the truth?'

Simon stared at his friend.

'There's simply no way to prove a scary story isn't true without facing it head on,' said Whippet.

Fear, thought Simon. *Yes. Fear is the key.*

'And besides,' continued Whippet as he started sketching again, 'old Armstrong isn't even a real sailor. He acts like some sort of pirate but his wooden leg is as fake as they come.'

Lucy had kept quiet while Whippet was talking but her frustration finally got the better of her.

'How can he fake a wooden leg?' asked Lucy, her face reddening in irritation. 'You haven't got a clue what you're talking about, Whippet.'

'I have too,' said Whippet, rising to the bait. 'I've drawn loads of pirates.'

'I know where to find it,' said Simon suddenly.

The others stopped squabbling and turned to face Simon.

'I wish I didn't, but I'm sure I know where it's hiding. You'd better follow me.'

And that said, Simon walked off, towards the path at the edge of the lake, and a fear he knew it was time to face.

CHAPTER 14

THE TOILET THAT TROLLS BUILT

Lucy and Whippet quickly fell into step
and joined Simon on the rough stone
path around Lake Shore. Simon had
set off anti-clockwise, walking

beside the water with his head bowed. He concentrated on trying to keep his breathing even but he was failing fast. The fear was already rising.

'Okay, I give up,' said Lucy. 'Where are we going?'

Simon's throat had grown incredibly dry. He opened his mouth to speak but the words had left him. Instead he simply pointed at the dark shape looming before them in the dusk. Whippet squinted.

'Turnaway Bridge? Oh, that place is really creepy. I've heard loads of horror stories about it,' said Whippet with far more enthusiasm than Simon thought was appropriate. 'But why do you think it's hiding there?'

Simon swallowed, felt his mouth loosen slightly at the exact same time his feet began to slow down.

'Because it's creepy. Everyone avoids it. Like you said, we've all heard the stories, Whippet. You know what I'm talking about.'

Simon stopped walking. His legs had seized up. They simply wouldn't move forwards. A cold panic was rising inside him.

Lucy grabbed him by the arm and hauled him onwards. Her strength was remarkable and Simon found himself being dragged on against his will.

'Stop it! What are you doing?' he said.

'Helping. Yes, this place used to be creepy, but that was a while ago. There's nothing to fear here now – except me, if you don't hurry up!'

As the three children arrived at the main support for Turnaway Bridge, Simon stopped and looked up in open-mouthed amazement. His family might have driven

over the bridge but he'd never, ever dared walk beneath it. Now he was within touching distance of it and he couldn't tear his eyes away.

The entire underside of the bridge, hidden from view and spanning the lake, was covered with hundreds of small stone gargoyles frozen in a variety of poses, from running to flying to playing Frisbee.

Every face was carved into a grin. It had the effect of making the underside of the bridge look like a bizarre sports club for imps.

Simon stared. His fear was now competing with another sensation. Fascination. Why had no one ever mentioned before what it looked like down here? It was bizarre, but cool, like something from the pages of **FREAKY**.

Lucy was also staring up at the gargoyles but her expression was calm.

'You've spent your whole life thinking this place was normal, right?'

Simon continued to gaze on in wonder. Lucy nodded.

'Yeah. Then one day a monster steals your sister,' she said, 'and all of a sudden you can't help but see the true Lake Shore. This is a very weird little town.'

Whippet called over to them. He was

pointing to the muddy ground near the water. Simon could see a clear set of fresh prints emerging and leading under the bridge.

'I've been such an idiot. I should have checked this out earlier,' said Lucy in irritation.

They followed the markings through the shadows and stopped dead. There, beneath Turnaway Bridge, tucked up tight against the main bridge support and hidden from view, in the last place anyone would ever want to live, someone had built a house.

'Nasty. What a dump,' said Whippet, wrinkling his nose in disgust. 'And what a pong. This place looks and smells like a public toilet for trolls.'

'Well spotted. It *was* used as a public toilet for trolls. I killed the last one six months ago,' said Lucy.

She didn't wink or smirk or laugh. Lucy appeared to be telling the truth.

'I told you it used to be creepy,' she said.

Simon suddenly felt excitement run through his veins like a bolt of electricity. He leaped forwards and plucked something soft from the ground. It was Ruby's cuddly Tyrannosaurus toy; minus one dinosaur nose.

Simon's heart lurched. They had to find a way inside but he was still wrestling with his fear. If the gargoyles hanging over their heads weren't freaky enough, the troll toilet was something else. Darkness looked like it had been painted across every inch of the rotten two-storey shack, and painted with a brush made from pure misery. Almost every one of the misshapen windows had been boarded up and the front door was secured with heavy chains and bulbous padlocks.

Simon crept towards the entrance. The prints came to an abrupt halt before the padlocked doors.

'My handiwork,' said Lucy. 'Trolls are absolutely fascinated by padlocks and can't bring themselves to damage them. They practically worship them. Plus, their fingers are too big to hold a key or a lockpick.'

'But if this place is locked up, I must be

wrong. It's not here. The creature's vanished,' said Simon.

Lucy laughed.

'Don't be such a half-wit. Look up,' she said, sorting through her big bag of tricks once more.

The boys did as they were told. There, in the gloomy half light, they could just make out a window ledge on the first floor where muddy claws had marked the surface. The boards covering the window looked like they'd been smashed open.

'How are we going to reach that?' said Whippet.

'We're not. We're not going up – we're going through,' said Lucy, pulling a strange tubular gadget from her backpack and slinging it up onto her shoulder. She squinted as she lined up a laser sight with the building's barred entrance.

'Stand back, boys. This Compressed-Air Bazooka is one of my own inventions

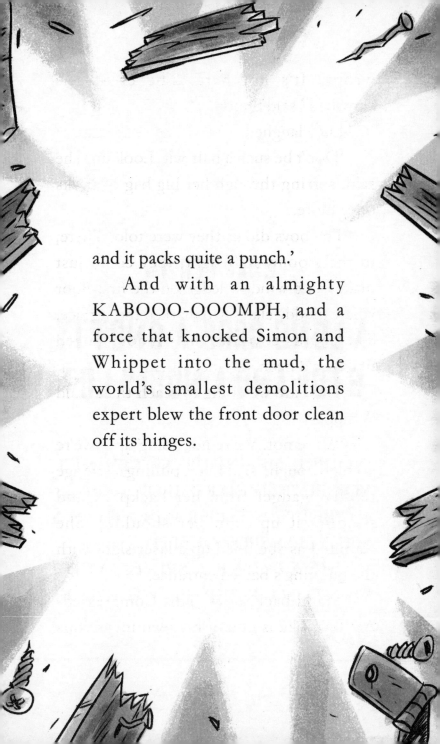

and it packs quite a punch.'

And with an almighty KABOOO-OOOMPH, and a force that knocked Simon and Whippet into the mud, the world's smallest demolitions expert blew the front door clean off its hinges.

CHAPTER 15

A LONG DROP, A SNOTTY STOP AND A NOSEY LOT

'YOU'RE OFF YOUR NUTTY NUT, YOU PINT-SIZED RAMBO!'

'BETTER TO BE RAMBO THAN A SPINELESS SPOT OF SPIT!'

'HEY, I HAVE A SPINE, AND I WANT TO KEEP IT WHERE IT

BELONGS – IN MY BACK AND IN ONE PIECE!'

'WELL, GOOD FOR YOU, BUT SOMEONE HAD TO GET US INSIDE!'

'BUT IT WAS *YOUR* PADLOCK! YOU COULD HAVE SIMPLY UNLOCKED IT!'

'TRUE! BUT THIS WAY WAS MUCH MORE FUN!'

Whippet and Lucy had been exchanging pleasantries of this sort for about ten minutes. As far as Simon was concerned, nobody had been hurt – the bazooka only fired AIR, after all – and Lucy had successfully found a way inside the building ... even if she could have simply unlocked it.

If the pair of them would just stop arguing, thought Simon, they could get on with rescuing Ruby.

Whippet, however, still had a few

thoughts on the subject.

'CRAZY, CRAZY GIRL! YOU'RE CRAZY, YOU ... YOU ... CRAZY GIRL!'

With this last award-winning insult, he ran out of steam and slouched off to sit on a stack of old planks. Unfortunately for him, the planks chose that precise moment to collapse.

For the first time, Lucy Shufflebottom laughed. She really, really laughed. Tears of delight poured down her cheeks as Whippet struggled to free himself from the wreckage.

Finally regaining her composure, Lucy bent over and held out her arm.

'Take ... take my ... hand ... ' she said, and gripping Whippet by the wrist she hauled him to his feet.

'I'm glad to see you two are making friends, but can we get on?' said Simon.

'You're right. Sorry, Mossy. Let's find

Ruby and get out of here. This place is one big smelly death trap,' said Whippet.

He had a point. The floor in front of them also seemed to have collapsed, leaving nothing but thin air between the trio and what looked like a very long plummet into a basement. The smell rising from beneath the floor was extremely pungent.

'Your trolls certainly made a mess in here,' said Whippet.

'I don't remember the floor being damaged when I locked the doors,' said Lucy, studying the edges of the hole. 'This is new. It wasn't trolls. Those big dumb lumps have hands like shovels, and this was dug with claws.'

Simon thought of the print they'd seen by the lake. It had definitely had claws.

A disgusting grunting snort erupted from the earthy tunnel. Simon peered into the hole.

'Did you hear that?'

'Yep, sounds like our target is home. Now is the time to strike,' said Lucy, with a smile like a shark just before it chews off your leg.

'Okay, so let's get down there,' said Simon.

He shot Whippet an encouraging smile.

'After you,' said Simon, hopefully.

'No, after you,' said Whippet, generously.

'No, no, no! YOU first, I insist,' said Simon, desperately.

'Oh, stop being pathetic,' said Lucy, dismissively.

She removed a grappling hook from her pack and tied it around the one and only solid-looking floor beam. Simon's mind boggled at the wonders and incredible gadgets that must be hidden in her massive rucksack. Lucy threw a long rope into the void, then jumped backwards and grappled her way down to the basement floor.

She was speedy, and yet Simon and Whippet managed to find an even quicker route.

While watching Lucy's professional descent, Whippet overbalanced. In a desperate attempt to steady himself he grabbed Simon – and together

they tumbled over the edge. The boys bounced and bounded down the drop like a runaway pinball, finally crash-landing at the bottom with a sickening SQWUMPH.

'Nice moves,' said Lucy as she fixed a head torch to the top of her explorer's hat, 'and it looks like you've found another clue.'

The clue, in which the boys had landed, was a pile of . . . well . . . it was sticky, thick, green and there was a lot of it.

'Bogies! I'm drowning in a sea of bogies!' said Whippet, his lips curled into a broad grin as he doggy-paddled free of the gloop. 'This is so gross it's . . . brilliant!'

'I think there could be something really wrong with you, Whippet,' said Simon. 'Anyway, it's more like a puddle than a sea of bogies.'

Whippet flicked a string of gloop from his fingers.

'Whichever way you look at it,' he said, 'only something with a really big nose could generate all this.'

'Exactly,' said Lucy. 'We're getting close, and our prey has left an easy trail to follow.'

Another horrendous roar burst from the corner of the basement, and the two boys jumped in shock. Lucy did not flinch. She swung

her head torch to the right and the beam glistened off a trail of glowing green gunk dribbling away towards a round brick tunnel.

'It's time this snotty horror met a sticky end,' said Lucy, setting off at a trot into the gloom with Simon and Whippet following behind.

Downwards they jogged, following the curves of the crumbling brick tunnel. Dripping pipes branched away into the darkness. The further and deeper the trio travelled from daylight, the gloomier it became.

Simon caught himself pondering just how far he'd come from his normal life and the safety of his own home. Every moment felt like a little cliffhanger, like the end of a chapter in a comic book. But where would the journey take them? he thought. His stomach tightened as he pictured his sister, lost in this horrible place, alone and scared. Whatever happened, he would find her. He had to find her.

Passing a junction in their path, Whippet suddenly skidded to a stop. Simon joined his friend and watched as Whippet blew a thick layer of dust from a metal plaque mounted on the wall. It appeared to be an old map of the tunnel system. A maze of overlapping pipes and flumes and vents and sluices looped left and right and up and down but they all led back into a large central chamber. The map was entitled, 'LAKE SHORE SEWER PUMPING STATION'.

'Yuk, we're in the sewers. That explains

LAKE SHORE SEWER
PUMPING STATION

the smell,' said Simon.

Whippet pointed at a small tunnel next to a large chamber on the map.

'We're standing right here, I think. So let me guess,' he continued, 'we're heading towards this chamber, right?'

Simon turned to look at the

splashes of green on the walls around them, then peered at the map again. Simon nodded to his friend. Whatever was waiting for them was just around the corner.

Lucy moved ahead into the main tunnel, creeping as stealthily as she could through the filthy water trickling beneath their feet. She directed her head torch upwards as their path opened into a huge cavern before them . . . and that's when things got really freaky.

The giant chamber was overflowing from floor to ceiling . . . with NOSES!

CHAPTER 16

THE LAIR OF THE BEAST

Lucy, Simon and Whippet stood before a mountain of stolen snouts. Thousands of concrete, plaster, cardboard, straw and plastic noses of every shape and size were piled high in dangerously large heaps, almost filling the cavernous area. What space remained was filled with piles of compost, mouldy rubbish and stolen kitchen supplies.

'Well . . . er . . . this is something you don't see every day,' said Whippet, giving new meaning to the word 'understatement'. He picked up a string of garlic from a nearby pile of rotting vegetables and tossed it to Simon.

As Simon caught it he felt a sense of

deep dread begin to rise inside him. He'd always hoped that if he ever managed to get over his fear of Turnaway Bridge and actually took a peek at what was beneath it, he'd discover he'd never really had anything to be afraid of. That it had just been his imagination playing tricks on him.

But down here, Simon had a very good reason to be afraid. This place was a whole new level of spooky. Simon shivered. He wasn't qualified to deal with mountains of noses piled amid a rotten sewer system, let alone tackle a monster. Neither was Whippet. They knew nothing about their enemy. Why was it living here? What was it after? Why did it want Ruby?

Where was Ruby?

Even with her weapons and bravery, Lucy was going to have a real battle on her hands.

But . . . perhaps there was something

Simon could do to help.

A suggestion niggled at the edge of Simon's mind. Just out of reach. It was a memory, he thought. Or an idea. A light at the end of the dark, stinky tunnel. It felt to Simon like his brain was connecting the dots, ever so slowly. As though he was trying to complete a jigsaw puzzle after his sister had thrown the box in the air, scattering the pieces. But before he could arrange his thoughts, a disgusting noise filled the chamber, like someone clearing their throat after a really, really bad cold.

Whippet's jaw dropped and Lucy drew her crossbows as a nearby pile of stolen noses crumbled into a nasal landslide and something huge bounded down the slope towards Simon. If he'd been scared before, he now fully understood the meaning of the word 'terror'.

The light from Lucy's head torch bounced off an impossible beast. Sliding and tumbling towards him was an armoured wall of black and purple muscle. It looked like the result of some horrible genetic experiment gone wrong – a rhinoceros crossed with a panther and a tank.

Most disgusting of all was its head. Beneath two tiny lidless black eyes and above a small mouth lined with razor-sharp teeth, the entire face was filled with a nose . . . a giant, snot-dribbling, wart-covered nose.

'What, in the name of **FREAKY** and **FEARLESS**, is that?' said Whippet, in horrified wonder.

'Trouble!' screamed Lucy. 'And it's after Simon!'

Simon realised with absolute confidence it was all over. In less than ten seconds he was going to meet his end at the claws of a giant monster which looked like it could have been ripped from the pages of his favourite comic. There was simply no way he could defend himself against such a beast.

His sense of dread threatened to swallow him whole. A pulsing tingle spread throughout him. Pure fear. Excitement. Danger. Imagination. His mind began to race ahead of him. His life didn't so much as flash past his eyes as fold, like the pages of a comic. The events of the last ten hours were all spread out before him like panels. This day, this whole experience, definitely qualified for what his dad had described as 'peculiar'. But now he realised he would never be able to share this particularly tall tale with his father.

That was it.

Tall tales.

Telling tales.

The queue for the comic shop, the reactions to his stories . . . Had that just been some one-off event? A lucky trick? Or was it something he could use? Could he do it again?

Simon stared into the horrifying open mouth and flared nostrils of the beast as it slid towards him and prepared to leap. This was it. He only had one tiny chance. But a story that could stop a monster in its tracks would need to be a very special, unique tale. Simon needed inspiration. He needed to make his dad proud . . .

I bet you could conjure an adventure from something as dull as a garden gnome.

Simon breathed in. Then out. An adventure from a garden gnome? Why not.

His mind raced. The Story formed itself.

Simon shut his eyes, and began to tell his tallest tale EVER . . .

The Day the Gnome Stood Still

Once upon a time, long, long ago, planet Earth was a peaceful place. This was way back, before cars or music or sports or arguments with siblings or demolition or all the noisy things that make modern life loud and interesting.

The only things living on our blue and green planet were gnomes. But not just garden gnomes. There were bedroom gnomes, bathroom gnomes, under-your-feet gnomes, just-outside-your-vision gnomes, how-did-you-get-up-there

gnomes – you name it, there was a gnome for it. They were absolutely everywhere but they did not disturb the peace. As a species made of stone, they were naturally slow moving and loved nothing better than standing still for hours on end, taking pleasure in the sound of their surroundings. The wind tickling its way through the long grass. The sun baking the soil dry until it cracked. The clapping applause of the thunder that followed a lightning bolt.

The gnomes were happy. Even the planet was quite happy.

Then those silly great dinosaurs arrived and the whole world went down the toilet!

See, the dinosaurs didn't care much for music. They took a lot more pleasure from simply stomping all over the place, thumping their tails, head-butting each other and gnashing their teeth. In fact, gnashing their teeth was the dinosaur equivalent of an Olympic sport and they were very,

very good at it. Especially when they saw something worth gnashing – which is where the gnomes came in.

The word 'massacre' isn't quite big enough, so let's just say that by the time the dinosaurs were finished, there were very few gnomes left in one piece. Those that did survive did so by hiding. Standing still didn't work. The dinosaurs called the gnomes who tried to hide by standing still 'ready meals'. The ones who tried to run were known as 'fast food'. (Dinosaur humour, it must be said, was not particularly refined.)

But then that silly great asteroid arrived and, thankfully for the gnomes, this time it was the dinosaurs that went down the toilet.

When the dust had settled, the gnomes came out of hiding. There were no more dinosaurs. Hooray. Then the silly great cavemen arrived.

They seemed to quite like music and spent much of their leisure time beating logs with wooden clubs, but those same wooden clubs turned out to be the caveman equivalent of gnashing teeth, and the result was more or less the same.

The gnomes went back into hiding.

Then homo sapiens arrived and got rid of all those pesky cavemen. Hooray. But these modern humans were too noisy for the gnomes, and there were also quite a lot of them. Millions, in fact. So the remaining gnomes went back into hiding, waiting for the next asteroid.

Until one day, hundreds of years and a few wars later, when an elderly man found a gnome in the wild. He took him home and placed him in his garden. He put a little fishing rod in the gnome's hands and smiled in delight. The man seemed to be extremely happy to have a gnome in his home, stealing his fish. And he wasn't alone. Soon everyone wanted a fish-stealing gnome, or a drinking-a-cup-of-tea gnome or a digging-a-hole gnome.

Standing still, the ultimate gnomish pastime, had become their greatest strength.

The planet was happy again, and for a while all was good. The gnomes were no longer being eaten or smashed or forced to hide.

Then the Snotticus Galavantia arrived.

A creature that stole noses. Including gnome noses. This time no gnome would be spared.

The gnomes knew it had to be stopped.

They knew.
They know.
They nose.
The nose.
Nose.

Simon stopped talking. He scratched his head. He'd completely lost his train of thought.

His tall, tall tale about short, short gnomes had ground to a halt.

He'd run out of story.

Oh dear.

CHAPTER 17

PLAN B

In the sewer pumping station beneath the troll toilet beneath the bridge, the silence seemed to swell. It was the sort of expectant silence you get when everyone thinks someone else is about to say something really important.

Simon blinked rapidly. He was struggling to comprehend what his eyes were telling him. Sitting amidst the scattered piles of broken noses were Lucy and Whippet, and beside them, was the monster. All three were sitting down and all three were looking up at him with the same intense expression of anticipation he'd seen on the faces of his friends outside Captain Armstrong's shop. The same expression Gubbin had pulled. They were listening so hard he could almost hear

them paying attention.

It had worked. Simon could barely believe it, but he had managed to entrance them all with a story. He had stopped them in their tracks – even the monster. The 'Snotticus Galavantia', as he had named it.

But that was about to change. Simon saw the creature shiver and realised his temporary hold over it had been broken. Whippet was still too dazed and distracted to notice the impending danger.

'Snotticus . . . great name, Mossy! But don't stop. What happened? Did the gnomes rise up in revenge?' asked Whippet.

Simon couldn't answer. The Snotticus had begun to crouch low, it muscles tensing as it readied itself to jump. Its lips curled into a rather nasty grin.

Thankfully for everyone concerned, Lucy managed to break the spell of Simon's

words with a frantic shake of her head, much like a wet dog drying itself after a bath. The little heroine snarled and leaped headlong into action.

'Story time is over, bozos,' she shouted, barging Simon and Whippet sideways just as the Snotticus pounced at them. The creature sailed through the air, missing them by millimetres, before crashing into a pile of rotten rubbish.

'Nice try, Simon, but I think it's time for Plan B!'

'Plan B? What's Plan B?' said Whippet, from his sprawled position on the floor.

'EXTREME VIOLENCE!' shouted Lucy and, levelling her crossbows at the monster, she fired twice in quick succession.

The bolts flew towards the beast's head but at the last moment the Snotticus twisted

to one side and the arrows shattered harmlessly on its armoured flank.

The monster sneered at Lucy, sucked up a huge noseful of air and snorted with all its might. As she dived out the way, a thick blast of snot whipped past, ripping the rucksack from her back and slapping it against the wall of the cavern with a disgusting *SHLUP*.

Lucy rolled to her feet in preparation for round two, but Simon grabbed her wrists before she could reload.

'Stop firing! Ruby's in here somewhere,

remember? You might hit her by accident!'

Without her bag of tricks the situation looked hopeless, even by Lucy's standards. But it is often in the face of true hopelessness that a hero will rise to meet the challenge. And when you can't find a hero, a weirdo like Whippet will do.

'HEY, you big Snotticus!' shouted Whippet, who had sneaked away and now stood in the mouth of a small tunnel leading off the main chamber. 'Are you hungry?'

The beast turned at the mention of its name. Simon frowned. The monster had recognised its own name. Could it be that Simon had actually used the creature's REAL name?

A tiny gnome's nose bounced harm-lessly off the Snotticus. It didn't have a lot of effect so Whippet threw another.

Clearly annoyed at the added insult of

being hit on the nose with a nose, the creature let out a horrible roar and chased after Whippet, who turned and disappeared inside the tunnel with a final warbling shout to his friends.

'Plan B didn't work . . . let's try Plan C!'

CHAPTER 18

PLAN C

'Er, what is Plan C?' said Simon.

'I've no idea . . . but listen,' said Lucy.

They stood in silence and strained to hear what was happening. Booming faintly around them, from deep within the overlapping tunnel system, came a series of confusing noises. Simon realised if he screwed his eyes shut he could separate two

distinct sounds. Over to his right he could hear the light *pat-pat-pat* of Whippet's running feet. And to his left was the heavy *tump-tump, tump-tump* of the Snotticus.

'He's trying to lose the monster,' said Lucy. If Simon hadn't known better he would have sworn Lucy almost looked impressed.

From over his shoulder, Simon heard a new sound. It was a familiar giggle, and well-loved. Turning and wading through the sea of noses, he rounded a corner and there, sitting happily amid a pile of rubbish, was Ruby. Simon clapped his hands in delight and raced towards her.

Ruby looked like she'd been bathing in sewage, but she didn't seem to care, and neither did Simon. He plucked his sister from the rubbish and gave her the biggest bear hug of her life. Perhaps his mum wasn't going to kill him after all.

'Hi, Si,' said Ruby. 'Have you met the big doggy with the funny nose? He's my new best friend.'

'Ruby, while it is true we've made a new friend today, it most certainly is not that monster. Forget it, okay?' said Simon, a huge grin of relief spread across his face. 'Once Whippet gets back we're leaving! All of us. We're going home!'

Right on cue Whippet emerged from one of the

higher tunnel entrances. 'Emerged' is the
wrong word. 'Propelled' is better. Actually,
he shot out of the tunnel like a cork from a
bottle, landing upside down on a towering
pile of noses and rolling unceremoniously
until he crashed at the feet of his friends.

Simon helped him upright.

'You found Ruby! That's great,' said
Whippet, brushing bits of rotting vegetable
from his hair.

'Whippet, how did you make your way
back out? I saw the map on the wall – those
tunnels looked like a maze,' said Simon.

Whippet looked a little sheepish.

'Yeah. They were. I got lost in about a

second and just kept running, hoping I'd find an exit. Then the Snotticus butted me in the bottom, HARD, and I flew through the air and, well, here I am,' said Whippet, grinning and dusting himself down.

'But still, you lost it, right? You gave the monster the slip?' said Simon hopefully.

Whippet rubbed his bottom again and shook his head.

'Not exactly. I think I might have

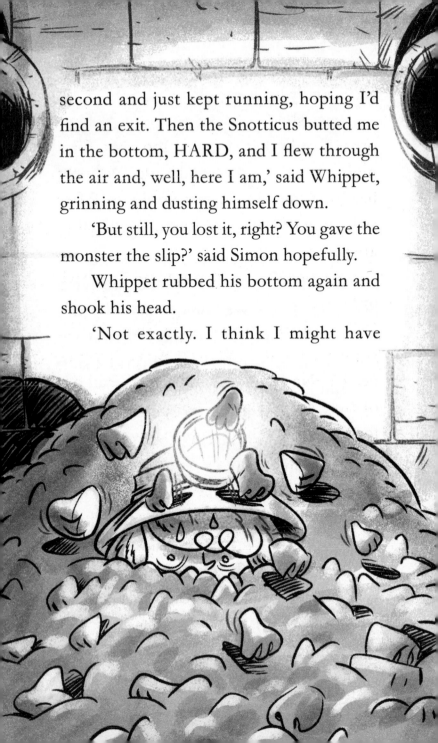

accidentally led it back here.'

Lucy shouted the word *idiot* (and some other words that sounded too rude for a nine year old to know) and hurled Whippet headfirst into the nearest nose pile. After switching off her head torch, she dived in after him.

A moment later, her head popped back up.

'What are you waiting for, Simon? Grab your sister and find cover! We're going to need a Plan D, and fast, before we run out of time and alphabet!' she said, pointing towards the tunnel Whippet had emerged from.

And with that Lucy disappeared from sight.

CHAPTER 19

TRAPPED

A tremendous noise erupted from the dozen tunnel entrances. It was a serious bellow. The bellow of a monster in a really bad mood.

Simon hugged Ruby tight and dived after Lucy. But he couldn't navigate the rubbish in the room without checking where he was going. Raising his head above

the surface of the noses, he watched in horror as the Snotticus hurtled into the cavern. It skittered to a halt amid the debris, and swung its giant nose left and right, sniffing and snuffling in confusion as it tried to locate its prey.

Ah, thought Simon, *it has to use its sense of smell to find us. Tiny ears. Tiny eyes. We can use that.*

Ducking back down, Simon gripped

Ruby's hand. He led them slowly away from the monster, carefully wading from one pile of old food to the next, making the minimum of sound and using the smell of the rotting fruit and vegetables to hide their own scent. Simon also made sure they only moved when the beast was turned away from their position. Gradually the pair worked their way towards one of the largest piles of undisturbed rubbish. It was a mountain of stolen kitchen goods and stinking peelings, and it blocked them completely from the monster's sight.

Lucy and Whippet had obviously had the same idea, as Simon found his friends hiding behind the rubbish. Lucy did not look happy, but Whippet was busy scribbling again, frantically drawing in his sketchbook. He looked up when Simon arrived.

'I think we're trapped, pal,' whispered

Whippet, pointing at the confines of their hidey-hole with his pencil. 'Pretty seriously trapped, actually.'

Simon looked at Lucy, secretly hoping she would suggest something daring and unpredictable that would save the day. However she seemed to be far more interested in reloading her crossbows than looking for an exit.

Whippet crawled over to Simon.

'I thought we were done for back there,' he said. 'But you stopped the Snotticus in its tracks.'

'Yeah, well,' replied Simon, 'it hasn't done us much good, has it?'

Whippet ran his fingers through his tangled black hair and studied his friend with a look of wonder.

'I've heard you tell plenty of stories, but that was . . . intense. It was like the only thing that mattered was listening. All I could think about were the words coming out of your mouth, and the pictures forming in my head,' said Whippet.

Simon smiled stupidly. He didn't know what to say. But Lucy did.

'Hypnosis!' she hissed at Simon, simultaneously flicking him on the forehead. Hard. 'You hypnotised us, Simon.'

Flick.

'You hypnotised ME and I do not like being hypnotised.'

Flick.

Simon raised his free hand to protect himself from the next attack.

'I don't know how to hypnotise people,' he objected. 'I've never done that in my life. Well, there was a sort of incident this morning, at the comic shop, but I can't really control it. Anyway, I don't see how that helps us get past this thing and out of here alive.'

Lucy looked down the sight of her bow.

'It won't. I haven't figured out how your skills can help the cause . . . not yet, anyway.'

Simon was about to ask what she meant but Lucy interrupted him.

'Besides, who said anything about getting past this thing? I don't go around problems, Simon. I go through them.'

'Getting around all these noses is going to be hard enough,' said Whippet. 'I mean, the Snotticus has obviously got a thing for collecting this stuff. But why?'

Lucy peeked around the pile to check on the creature. She ducked back and held a finger to her lips.

'Remember earlier how you suggested it was acting like a magpie?' she whispered. 'Well, it's got a disgustingly big nose, so perhaps it just loves collecting noses. Or perhaps it hates them. Who knows? Monsters don't think the way we do. You can't figure them out like that. I don't even bother trying.'

Simon chewed on his lip as Lucy continued to work on her crossbows. Whippet had returned to his sketchbook and was frantically drawing.

'Whatever the reason, it's obviously obsessed,' she said, 'and as for all this other junk, well, what did it steal?'

Simon looked around.

'Rubbish,' he said.

'Yes,' said Lucy, 'but not just rubbish.'

She plucked a jar from the pile and threw it to Simon. The label on the pot read 'chilli powder'.

'Simon, this thing's been raiding kitchens all over town and stealing everything stinky it could find. Mouldy fruit and veg, old meat and fish, herbs, spices, anything with a good whiff. I think it's addicted to smelly stuff, which is probably why it made a home for itself in the sewer. It's even smellier down here than up above in the troll's toilet.'

Simon studied the jar again. Ruby tugged at his sleeve.

'Look, are we going home or not, Si?' she asked. 'Or can I go play with the dog?'

Simon looked down at his sister, the sole reason he was facing off against a nightmarish monster.

'Forget the noses and rubbish – why did it take Ruby? It hasn't stolen HER nose,' whispered Simon.

Lucy's expression changed. She looked almost worried.

'I think she was bait.'

'Bait for what?' said Whippet. He'd finally stopped drawing. Simon noticed the pencil had been worn down to a tiny nub.

But before Lucy could answer, the room began to shake. The monster had unleashed another mighty bellow as it hunted in vain for Simon and the others. The noise sent vibrations through the piles of junk and a section of their hiding place collapsed, covering them in debris.

As they picked their way clear of the mess, Whippet started to gag, and scrape at his tongue. He was covered in a fine powder of white crystals, which had turned his black hair almost grey.

'Ah, ugh, salt! Gah! I've got salt in my mouth! Yuk!' he moaned.

Simon stopped. There it was – the tiniest glimmer

of an idea, one that was every bit as crazy as their other plans. Not salt but . . . yes. It could work.

First he checked his right-hand pocket. He grinned in relief. Thankfully they were still there.

Simon began to ferret through the piles of junk around them. Lucy watched him work.

'What are you looking for?' she asked.

Simon ignored her and continued to search. Finally spotting his prize, he gripped a large wooden pepper grinder that was lying on its side, and raised it so the others could see.

'Pepper! I was looking for pepper. This, unless I'm mistaken, is the ultimate weapon against a giant nose.'

Simon pulled out his pack of amusingly shaped balloons – the packet that had failed

to captivate the kids in the comic shop queue.

'By combining this ingredient with these balloons, I think we can deliver a message the Snotticus will never forget,' said Simon. 'First, we're going to need to find a lot more of these pepper grinders, and then . . .'

And then the gang huddled together to listen as Simon explained his last-ditch, everything-and-the-kitchen-sink, this-had-really-better-work, fingers-and-toes-crossed, Plan D!

CHAPTER 20

PLAN D

The Snotticus paced back and forth, sniffing and snuffling in annoyance. It couldn't detect a single smell of its quarry over the stink of its own home. It couldn't hear them. It couldn't see them. But it knew they were still in the cavern chamber.

On the filthy breeze, it heard a whisper. The beast turned its head to track the noise.

'One, two, three . . . and . . .'

At once Simon and Whippet erupted from the two piles of rubbish either side of the Snotticus. They had stealthily worked their way right up to the beast, each boy holding an inflated balloon. Simon's was shaped like a sumo wrestler and Whippet was gripping a jolly round pig.

The monster reared backwards in surprise. Before it could react further, there was another disturbance. Rising from

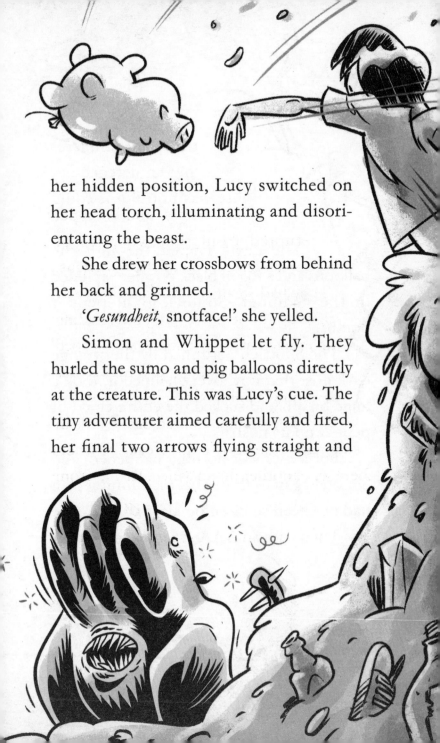

her hidden position, Lucy switched on her head torch, illuminating and disorientating the beast.

She drew her crossbows from behind her back and grinned.

'*Gesundheit*, snotface!' she yelled.

Simon and Whippet let fly. They hurled the sumo and pig balloons directly at the creature. This was Lucy's cue. The tiny adventurer aimed carefully and fired, her final two arrows flying straight and true. The monster turned in defence but there was nothing it could do.

The darts ripped through the balloons and a fog of black powder exploded in the chamber. Simon's giant pepper bombs.

The Snotticus, stunned by the strange dark mist that now overwhelmed it, took a huge breath and sucked the entire cloud of pepper up its nostrils.

For a moment nothing happened, and Simon began to think that his cunning plan had not been so cunning after all.

Then with an AAA . . . and an AAAAA

. . . and an AAAAAAAAAA. . .
and an AAAAAAAAAAAA-
AAAAAACHOOOOOOOO-
OOOOOO, the Snotticus
released a record-breaking sneeze
and disappeared behind a tidal
wave of snot.

A gazillion pea-green bogeys
filled the room, washing Lucy,
Whippet and Ruby off their feet.
Simon had just enough time to
regret not thinking Plan D all the
way through, before he was hit by
the gross and salty wave.

As the waist-high wash settled across the chamber, the brave survivors slowly staggered to their feet, coughing and spluttering. Whippet whooped and let out a laugh of triumph. He patted his pockets absent-mindedly and gasped in horror, then dived back into the rubbish.

Lucy waded over to where the Snotticus had last been standing. Her hands dug through the putrid slop.

'Total nasal disintegration,' she said in amazement. 'I've never seen it before ... but I could've beaten it on my own. You do know that, right?'

'Oh, I believe you,' said Simon, as he plucked Ruby from the gloop. She was desperately trying to inflate the last of the novelty balloons. Simon smiled. Even surrounded by all this mess and madness his sister was able to happily distract herself with an inflatable penguin. She didn't seem in the slightest bit bothered about being kidnapped by the Snotticus that they had just destroyed. Simon turned to Lucy, who was digging her huge backpack out of the rubbish.

'Where are you going?' he asked.

'Home. We won, it lost. And it's getting late, you know. Especially for your sister.'

'What? You can't just go. I've got questions. Lots of questions! You said Ruby was bait . . . bait for what?'

Lucy shouldered her rucksack and pointed a finger at Simon.

'For you, of course. I think the Snotticus knew you were a threat, somehow, and
it snatched your sister in order to draw you
out, to lead you here to your doom. It might
have worked too, but I joined the party. The
monsters, they all . . . know me. They know
what I'm capable of. If you ask me, the
Snotticus got a big whiff of my scent and it
ran for the hills. That's why it tried to cover
its tracks at the lake. It was hiding from me.'

Simon scratched his head. The monster
had seemed to be looking for something in
Simon's garden, before it grabbed Ruby.
Could it have been searching for Simon all
along? And there was another even weirder
issue. He'd told the children in the comic
queue that the Snotticus was a child-stealing
beast. Bred for one purpose – to kidnap
children.

Which was exactly what it had done.

Simon swallowed. He . . . he hadn't

given it the idea . . . had he?

Simon opened his mouth to ask but Lucy interrupted.

'No. No more questions. Don't even think about asking me how you managed to hypnotise a monster, or me for that matter, because I don't have the slightest clue. I do, however, intend to find out.'

Simon stuffed his hands in his pockets. His fingers closed around a small soggy piece of paper. It was the email address his dad had given him that morning. The story of how he beat the Snotticus was going to make an amazing first email, although he secretly doubted his dad was going to believe him. There was strange, and there was *strange*, and then there was a tale of a monster running around stealing noses and nabbing children.

'So it's all over.'

Lucy had reached the tunnel entrance.

She stopped, turned and shook her head.

'Not even close, Fearless,' she answered. 'When I said this town was strange, I meant it. Our world, and the world where that monster came from . . . they're much, much closer than you realise. And it looks like the doorway has been left wide open to whatever feels like stepping through.'

'Er . . . did you just call me Fearless?' asked Simon.

Lucy gave a rare grin.

'I think it's time for a new nickname. Your balloon plan back there was both

brave and stupid. Makes you pretty Fearless in my book.'

At that precise moment Whippet reappeared. He staggered slowly towards Simon like a snotty ghoul, his outstretched hands clutching his dripping notebook. Simon took the book gingerly from him as his friend sank to his knees in exhaustion.

'Found it,' he gurgled.

Lucy watched him and sighed.

'But your pal, Whippet,' she continued, 'well, that daft boy will only ever be Freaky. You boys have a lot to learn,' she said, trudging slowly away, her voice echoing back over her shoulder as she moved further up the tunnel. Then she paused, but didn't turn.

'Oh, one final thought: you two can believe what you like, but Captain Armstrong really IS a pirate. I've seen him in action. The real question to ask is why would a famous pirate sell comics for a living?'

And then the world's smallest explorer waded out of the chamber.

'See you later, Fearless.'

Simon watched her leave with a mixture of relief and disappointment. For a heavily armed lunatic who could probably kill him with her thumb, when it came to the crunch, she was pretty cool.

Whippet collapsed in a sticky heap beside his friend.

'Did you dive back in, just for this?' said Simon in disbelief.

'Never leave a good sketch behind, that's my motto,' said Whippet.

He turned to look around the chamber in confusion.

'Hey, where did Lucy go?'

CHAPTER 21

WHITE LIES FOR BEGINNERS

Much later, long after Simon and Ruby had returned home, after their mother had finally stopped hugging them and stopped shouting at them, long after they'd told a great big fib about where they'd been and why they were covered in gallons of indescribably disgusting filth, and after they'd showered to get rid of the gallons of indescribably disgusting filth . . . long after all that, Simon finally flopped on to his bed. He was armed with everything he needed to end the day in style: a big bag of sweets and his latest issue of **FEARLESS**. But first he needed to check in with Whippet.

Simon picked up the walkie-talkie he kept close to hand for just these sorts of eventuality, and buzzed his best friend in the whole world.

There was a short pause. Whippet's voice crackled back from the receiver. From the chewing sound, Simon deduced that Whippet was also enjoying a late-night

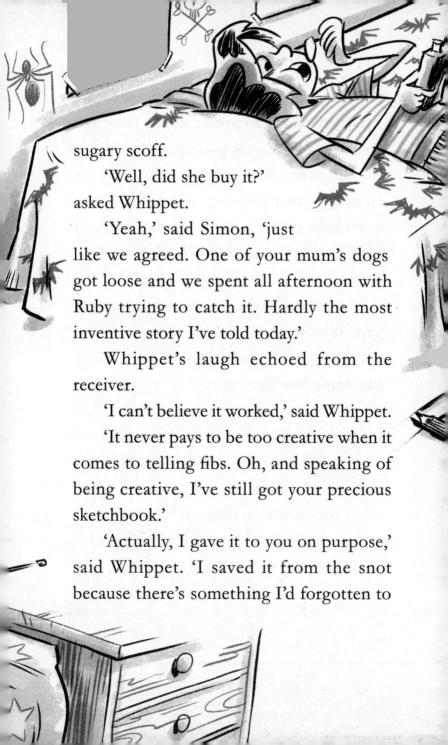

sugary scoff.

'Well, did she buy it?'
asked Whippet.

'Yeah,' said Simon, 'just
like we agreed. One of your mum's dogs
got loose and we spent all afternoon with
Ruby trying to catch it. Hardly the most
inventive story I've told today.'

Whippet's laugh echoed from the
receiver.

'I can't believe it worked,' said Whippet.

'It never pays to be too creative when it
comes to telling fibs. Oh, and speaking of
being creative, I've still got your precious
sketchbook.'

'Actually, I gave it to you on purpose,'
said Whippet. 'I saved it from the snot
because there's something I'd forgotten to

show you. A picture I finished when we were trapped in the sewer. It was inspired by that weird animal you met. You know, the one outside the castle?'

Simon reached over and grabbed the sketchbook lying on top of his new issue of **FREAKY**. Whippet sounded thoughtful as he spoke.

'I'd had a go at drawing it when we were in your treehouse, and again when we were sitting by the lake, but my pictures were hopeless. Maybe fear is inspiring or something, because after my run-in with the Snotticus, I knew exactly what to draw.'

Simon started flicking through the sketches. The walkie-talkie crackled again.

'Listen, I'd better go, Mossy. Mum's on the warpath about the damage to the garden and I'm still pretty sore from where that stupid creature headbutted me. Weirdest thing too – it sort of stung at the time, but in the strangest way. Almost felt like a paper cut.'

Simon wrinkled his brow.

'What?' he asked.

'Yeah, the more I think about it, for a split-second it felt exactly like getting a paper cut. And it tingled like mad. What a day, eh? This is why I don't leave the house.'

Simon nodded. Whippet might have a point there.

'Anyway, night, pal. See you tomorrow,' said Whippet.

The walkie-talkie fell silent and the cogs in Simon's mind began to turn. Whippet's last words had joined a ridiculously long queue of confusing recollections, which were slowly merging into one big flashback of the day's madness. He and Whippet had followed clues, tracked a kidnapper, made friends with a tiny lunatic, discovered a troll toilet, rescued his sister from a sewer and beaten a monster with pepper bombs and crossbow bolts. Simon was exhausted just thinking about it.

He turned to the last entry in the sketchbook. Simon stared at Whippet's final drawing and frowned. There, filling the page from corner to corner, captured in all its glory, was the small, nervous-looking, monkey-like creature from Castle Fearless, the strange animal he'd encountered at the beginning of a day packed with strange encounters. Gubbin.

And the picture was perfect.

How is this possible? wondered Simon. He'd barely described the creature to Whippet, and yet his friend had been able to draw it as if he'd been there himself. The image was so good it was almost like looking at a photograph.

Simon gave a huge yawn. Whippet's unnatural talent with a pencil was a mystery that would have to wait. He dropped the sketchbook, picked up the comic by his bed and flicked off the main light. The stars on his ceiling shone down with a warm glow.

The world seems pretty odd and that's because it is odd, echoed the memory of his dad's words.

You have a lot to learn, came Lucy's parting message.

Uh-huh, thought Simon. *No kidding.*

Simon switched on his pocket torch, ducked his head beneath his duvet and opened the pages of **FEARLESS**. His battle with the Snotticus had given him a new appreciation of the stories in the comic. Especially the heroes. Simon had been frightened and confused but when he'd had no choice, he'd faced his fears and looked them square in the eye, or in the case of Turnaway Bridge, square in the gargoyle. Simon had always loved creating his own adventures and had often dreamed of having one for real, and today he had finally lived and survived one.

He felt inspired. The summer holiday lay ahead. Perhaps there was enough time for his previously boring town to present him with another adventure. Despite the day having been filled to the brim and overflowing with craziness, Simon realised he was hungry for more.

He was also just plain hungry and so, digging his hand into the open bag of fruit chews that lay beside him, Simon guzzled a mouthful of treats, opened his comic, and began to read.

A muffled, warbling cry rose from beneath Simon's duvet. He gripped the comic so hard he almost tore the pages. Staring at the panels, he was unable to believe his eyes. Forget Whippet's drawing of Gubbin, thought Simon. This was the real deal. This put the freak into **FREAKY** and the fear into **FEARLESS**.

For the chef... the comic chef... the fictional chef... the *Batty Beasts* chef from his comic... that chef was standing on top of the Snotticus.

Their Snotticus.

And in that moment Simon realised that this was one mystery that would not keep until his dad got back. Simon, Whippet and Lucy were in for a very busy summer.

MOST ASSUREDLY NOT THE END!

COMING SOON . . .

The Art of Being a Freak

Is Lake Shore safe?

Simon and Whippet are't sure where the
Snotticus came from or what else might be
out there — and they haven't seen Lucy
in weeks. Where on earth is she?

And could Whippet be developing
a superpower of his own?

ROBIN ETHERINGTON, as one half of The Etherington Brothers, has written three graphic novels that have been nominated for an array of awards. He has also produced comic stories for bestselling brands like Star Wars, Transformers, Wallace and Gromit, The Dandy, Kung Fu Panda and How to Train Your Dragon as well as writing for animation and film. Robin regularly tours schools and book festivals with events in the UK and abroad. Through energetic, laughter-filled Q&A sessions he loves to share his passion for reading, writing, art and the power of imagination. *Freaky & Fearless* is his first novel series.

JAN BIELECKI has studied both comics and illustration and has co-created two critically acclaimed graphic novels in Swedish. He is also a prolific children's book illustrator and his work has been published in Sweden, the UK and France. He has illustrated the *Wrestling Trolls* series for Hot Key Books. He would rather draw than describe himself:

Thank you for choosing a Piccadilly Press book.

If you would like to know more about our authors, our books or if you'd just like to know what we're up to, you can find us online.

www.piccadillypress.co.uk

You can also find us on:

We hope to see you soon!